Seven And an Eighth

The Journeys of Ignomatius

Retta Flagg

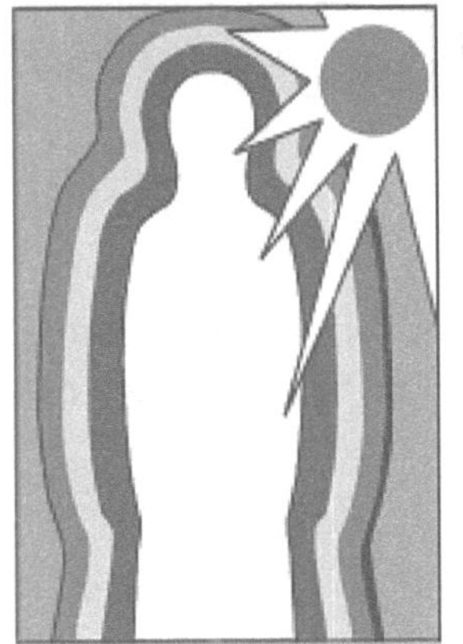

*Integrated
Spirit
Publishing*

Acknowledgements:

First on my list is my partner, Crystal Doll, editor in chief, cook, and a patient and wise listener. We have walked our spiritual path together for 25 years.

This book would not have been born without the encouragement and advice of my spiritual teacher, Samuel (www.discoversamuel.com) and the woman who channels him, Lea Schultz.

My beta test readers were fantastic and I owe so much to them for making my book the best it could be. A million thanks to Angela Curtis, Adam Curtis, Brenda Curtis, Saeeda Hafiz, Jana Thompson, Bree Hawthorne, Chris Boone, Laura Reed, and David Gosselyn. Jana wins the prize for coming up with the title. Saeeda was, and continues to be, a great mentor and cheerleader during my writing and publishing process.

Thanks to all who contributed in making my book happen: Gil Hoffman rode in like a knight in shining armor to format my book; Chris Boone, designer extraordinaire, designed the book cover; Jan Boone for embodying my vision in her design for the cover art; Marion Kee for last minute proofreading; contributors to my GoFundMe. Every contribution made a difference in helping me launch this book. If I've forgotten to acknowledge someone, please forgive me. You still get kudos from the Universe and my heart.

I would also like to thank the Seven Sisters for their constant companionship while I wrote the book. Characters tend to take on a life of their own and live in your head just as much as family and friends.

Introduction

There is an ancient Greek legend about seven sisters who were the offspring of Atlas and Plieone. The true story of the sisters reveals the feminine nature of the Divine and the introduction of the ancient mysteries into human consciousness. The mythological stories cover briefly what each of the seven sisters did in their lives here on Earth. They dallied with gods and men. Had children and adventures and then they were tossed into the heavens by Zeus allegedly to avoid the attentions of the great hunter, Orion. They travel through the night as the constellation Pleiades.

The fact that a version of the story of the seven sisters exists in many of the ancient cultures suggests that their teachings had an impact on the entire mass consciousness of that time. They were called the Sibittu in Mesopotameia and Babylonia. In India, they were the Krittikas. In China they were the Ch'i Kutzu or the Seven Young Ladies. In New Zealand, they were called the Matakari. In Australia, they were the Maya-Maya. In Egypt, they were the Seven Hathors. In Polynesia, they were the Meamei.

Many of the Avatars of human history followed the initiatory path during their lives: Jesus, Mohamed, Apollo, and Buddha are some of the well-known avatars of our history. The fact that there have been female avatars in human history has been overlooked in most versions of history. Once female scholars started studying ancient writings, a whole new perspective came to light: the main deities of ancient history were female in nature. In our patriarchal society, the feminine aspect of the Divine has been buried in our consciousness, and it takes great initiative and daring to reconnect with the Female Divine Oneness that is rooted in our ancient archetypes.

While many people call the Divine Matrix, God or Goddess, neither of these words captures the true essence of that energy which generates our universe and those beyond. While God and Goddess as representations of feminine creation energy and masculine manifestation energy hold the patterns of the duality of our existence, the Source of creation is beyond words to conceptualize and exists in multiple layers of creation energy.

Everything around us and within us is Source. We are expressions of Source. To find meaning and connection to the Divine, we need only to look within and recognize the Oneness of all creation. While this sounds simple, it is a process that crosses lifetimes of experience and even dimensions of existence.

Prologue

I stand upon the bow of the tour boat with the murky waters of the Ganges flowing beneath my feet. As I stare at the water, I superimpose the memory of standing in the heavens while watching Shiva pour the radiance of Ganga onto the Earth, dividing into four rivers of healing light. At that time, I so wanted to be bathed in the light of Ganga as it embodied in the waters of the Ganges. Now I cannot even touch the polluted river before me without fear of being exposed to dangerous bacteria. Yet deep within the waters, I still sense the heart of spiritual union that imbues India with that special connection to Source that we call God.

Light is dancing in my eyes as the reflection of the sun bursts out on the surface of the water. The bright light before me sends me deeper into the memories of my spiritual journey. I started that journey in the dark subconscious domain of the spirit and was transported by the light of love into dimensions that continue to challenge my understanding of the world and beyond.

Chapter One

"My touch is both a curse to a few and a gift to others."
The Hooded One

In the long ago times of human consciousness, the sacred touch of the Divine Oneness created seven sisters who came to Earth to teach the wonder and joy of being Light Beings in physical form. It is said that they were a result of the union of Atlas and Plieone, but the truth of their entering into the Earth Plane is a story that will take the human mind back to its origins and forward into its future. The Seven Sisters were the embodiment of those truths and this is their story as seen through my eyes.

Who am I? I am known as Ignomatius to the ones who chose me to tell their story. I feel as if there is a geas laid upon me that compels me to write about my experiences with these Beings of Light. Gather your courage and let go of your preconceptions as you join with me on this journey.

***

This summer has been wet and chilly. I am sitting in my back room looking out the picture window and enjoying the sun as it briefly illuminates the trees and lawn. A patch of light holds the bright color of a cardinal as it feeds on the emerald lawn. My eyes follow the splash of color as it moves in its quest for a late afternoon snack. The shadows and light play in the leaves of the trees as the wind from an approaching storm blows across the yard.

I put my book to the side as I enjoy the beauty before me. Perhaps I will find the meaning I have been looking for in the simplicity of the life cycle of my back yard.

The discarded book is a compilation of Greek legends and stories. For the last several years, I have been searching for spiritual meaning: meditation groups, gurus, channeled entities, A Course in Miracles, and even sweat lodges. While I have had moments of wonder and connection, no one path has emerged that feeds the yearning in my heart. I thought the drama of the Greek gods and goddesses might entertain me through another rainy weekend but the author of this book was too literal in his interpretation of the gods.

Surely there was some basis for the powers of the gods described in the legends. Did the gods once walk the earth or was it just stories meant to feed the imagination? My favorite theory was of some kind of interdimensional beings who had visited our planet.

As I ponder my spiritual path, the clouds move in and hide the late afternoon sun. As the gloomy darkness gathers around me, my thoughts turn to the dream that has been haunting me. I can only remember bits and pieces, but I know it had recurred several nights a week. My memory holds visions of a narrow, winding stairway and a hooded figure leading me deeper into the darkness. I know I should be afraid as images of the hooded figure flash through my memory, but for some reason I am very attracted by what lay at the bottom of the steps.

I return my attention to the room before me as lightning flashes and the storm starts in earnest. No brilliantly colored birds are on the lawn now. I turn on the lights and go to prepare my dinner. My spiritual answers will have to wait for yet another day.

***

We are going down stairs. It is dark and damp and quiet except for my rambling. I seem to be chattering incessantly to the figure before me. I have seen her before in my dreams a hundred times, beckoning me to follow. This is the path to the Mysteries, I am sure. A lifetime spent searching and now, at last, I am here. She motions for me to stop and puts her finger to her lips in a gesture of silence and then points. I look in the direction that she is pointing and see . . . nothing. We wait with her arm raised and directed towards something I cannot see. Nothing happens. I begin to doubt myself and the situation. Is this another dead end?

She drops her arm and turns to me. I don't even know if it is a she, I can't really tell. I have always referred to it as "she" in my dreams. In the darkness something brushes my forehead and I feel a great pain, like the skin on my forehead is being peeled away. I gasp and fall back to sit on the step behind me, sure that she's going to kill me! I clutch my head and as the pain subsides, I feel no blood. Still breathing heavily, I take my hands away in the dark and see them outlined in light. It is so odd that for a moment I just simply stare at them, unable to grasp or process anything.

I finally look up and there is light everywhere, but not light. My mind is reeling. I look at the figure in front of me and it glows with life, a powerful beacon that is somehow connected to everything around it. I can barely process the meaning of it all. Then I see her hands reaching toward me again and I tremble at her touch, in fear of how I will be transformed again. Her hands cover my ears and it feels like a bolt of lightning flashes through my brain. I can literally see all the structures: the pineal gland and the pituitary gland are spinning. The amygdala is lit up.

All of a sudden I can hear her voice in my head! It is booming and loud and I am afraid.

"You have been blind and deaf too long. It is time for you to see and hear the full spectrum of the world around you."

"Please," I beg her, "don't do anything else. These gifts of telepathy and seeing auras are beyond what I can hold." I sense a sad smile on her face even though I cannot see it.

Again she speaks. *"You have searched for this for years and now that you are here, you would deny what you have searched for? How human. It is good for you that I have learned compassion, for this is just the beginning of the journey and already you are overwhelmed."*

Again her hand comes toward me and I am so overcome with fear that I am paralyzed. This is not the treasure I had expected, not what I had been searching for at all. I hear her voice reply, *"Or is it?"* Then her hand touches me and I sink into oblivion. Sweet oblivion.

***

I hear a steady down pouring of rain. We have had much too much rain lately. I shake my head. Something about my head . . . then I remember my dream of last night. Was it really a dream? It felt so real. I can still remember the pain, then the lights and then her voice inside my head. It all comes back and I bolt out of bed as if by standing I can make the dream feel more unreal. I can still feel the pressure of her touch. Who is this hooded woman?

9

I fall to my knees when her voice answers me in my head: *"I am one who has been lost in time and my journey has led me to you."*

I am awake. This is not a dream and her voice is still in my head.

"And hearing my voice is the least of the work we have to do together, Ignomatius."

I try breathing deeply and get up and decide that a cup of tea will help me feel more normal.

My head remains silent, so I proceed to the kitchen and prepare the water and the teacup. It's a weekend morning. No voice in my head yet, so I keep focused on my breathing and my tea preparations. First, boil the water. Put the loose leaf tea into the pot, English breakfast this morning. Let it brew for a full five minutes to be nice and strong. I am pacing back and forth as I wait. My Scottish heritage comes out when the tea is finally ready and I add lots of sugar and cream. I go out to the family room in the back of the house to watch the morning light on the trees. I sip my tea.

"A perfect cup of tea this morning."

I nearly spill the tea all over myself.

"You might as well relax. Why don't you meditate and see what we can do?"

I stubbornly sip on my tea and stare at the yard. She may be in my head, but I can pretend to have some semblance of control. I'm sure I am stark raving mad. My friends were right about dabbling in esoteric mumbo jumbo, it clearly is dangerous.

I sense a sad smile from her and I can feel the emotion behind it. Do I really want to know?

"What do you want to know?"

I want to know the meaning of life. And how to get the love that I want and need. And what is God's plan? I am rambling again like I was in my dream last night. It disturbs me even more because it so parallels my experience in my dreams. Maybe I am still asleep.

***

Sleep has been difficult the last few days. I am afraid that she will appear in my dreams again. Then I am afraid that she will not appear in my dreams again. I don't know which one scares me more. The whole experience is beyond anything that I've ever known. Am I losing my mind or is this real? Voices talking in your head are a sign of being crazy, but her voice is so calming. Her presence touches me in ways that I cannot describe.

***

I am dreaming again. I know this is a dream. I have dreamt it many times. I am following the hooded figure down the steps. Down . . .down. . . they spiral down into the darkness and I follow her. Like a moth to a flame, I am drawn deeper into her light. I can see the lines of light radiating from her through the darkness. This is different from my other dreams. I nearly stumble on a step. A surge of energy flows through me as I remember my last dream and her touch, both the pain and the gentle love. Perhaps I can wake up before she touches me again. I stop and struggle to wake up. She turns to me. She waits. I can feel her waiting just as if I was feeling myself wait. There is that sense of a sad smile again and I stop trying to wake up. Her sadness draws me on even more than the light. Such a burden to bear.

Her voice is in my head again. *"Mankind has hungered for my touch down through the ages. And you fear that touch!"*

I am not sure if it is a gift or a curse.

"I can hear your thoughts. My touch is both a curse to a few and a gift to others. You need not fear me. We have planned this connection several lifetimes ago. You will use this gift to journey beyond your imagination."

I focus on my feet as we walk down. . . down. It is too much to focus on the hooded figure that I follow. She is more, so much more, than I had ever dreamed. I can feel her power when she talks to me. It's like stepping into a waterfall and being pummeled by the water.

"Ah, but what do you find when you walk through the waterfall?"

I continue on as if my thoughts were my own and as if my mind was not being read like an open book.

When we finally reach the bottom, she turns to look at me and slowly raises her arm to point. My eyes follow to where her arm points, but this time it is as though my whole being follows to where she has pointed. I am transported into the point of light at the tip of her fingers. As I gaze upon it, I am engulfed by it. I am. . . I am. . . I am something, someone else. So big. So very big. My sense of identity fades away.

***

Maia was a creature of the air. She drifted about the Earth Plane for a long time vaguely aware of the energies and happenings below her as she passed over land and water. Her form radiated colors as she changed with each thought that went through her mind. Mind was still new to her, as was form. It took a while to get used to being in form. Time as a linear flow was a new experience to her and now she needed time to gather herself together before she took up her actual work.

Maia was the first sister of the Pleiades to enter the Earth Plane. She was the embodiment of "Will To Be". "Will To Be" is the first aspect of Source. "Will To Be" created the Heavens and the Earth, it was the breath that created life. Maia was basic life force energy in its purest form capable of maintaining identity and consciousness. She drifted in her pure state for eons before she coalesced into a feminine being to take up her work with the peoples of the evolving Earth.

Her thoughts started taking form around her. At first, they were the rain, and the clouds, and the lightning that travels in the sky. Then they were little birds that flew down to the earth and back up again, totally changed by their experience. There was much to think about in form. It was disconcerting. It required time. She floated.

Maia was the pure, molten energy of fire. Her energy flowed as vast glowing waves of heat and liquefied metals. She was star energy encapsulated in earth form, she was "Will To Be" in primal fire form. Her thoughts beat as waves upon the planet's crust around her. Mountains moved. Earthquakes swallowed whole areas of land. She created her own equilibrium by releasing thoughts up to the surface that emerged as violent volcanoes. Oh, the power and the glory of fire as it flowed in the inner heart of the Earth: it intoxicated her soul. As elemental power on Earth, when her thoughts flowed, the planet changed. Maia took the form of fire as it was shaped by land around her, long, slow patterns of flowing energy that erupted to the surface in great release. She flowed like magma being released from the center of the earth.

Maia was water, endless, boundless water. Her depths were immeasurable. Her body was fluid. Her thoughts flowed through her. There were no boundaries or limitations of being. She was

"Will To Be" as it manifested in complete adaptability. Nothing could withstand her endless touch. All things around her were changed by contact with the fluidity of her being.

There were other beings in the water, in her essence. Some were so small as to be hardly felt within the flow of her consciousness. Others swam through the waters as their behemoth bulk left wakes behind them in both the water and her consciousness. Her essence buoyed them up in their environment. She nurtured them and they lived and died within the matrix of her form as water.

Maia was earth. She was the solidity of the rocks. She was the breaking down of the rocks into soil. She was the growth of the soil into trees. She was the bark of the trees being ingested and becoming earth on four legs. Earth was solid and yet it changed as constantly as the air, water, and fire. Earth was the weight of her thoughts upon her. Earth became the expression of her thoughts as she learned form.

Maia was spirit. Her Spirit and consciousness reached out to the elements and shaped them into being. Spirit touched fire that was Maia and fire became basic life energy. Spirit touched earth that was Maia and earth became flesh and bone. Spirit touched air that was Maia and breath animated the flesh and bone. Spirit touched water that was Maia and the waters of the earth flowed through the veins of flesh and bone. Spirit and consciousness imbued all form that was Maia and was glorified in her essence.

***

The scene shifts dramatically and I am breathless as I stand within a stone circle, no longer a goddess but a witness to the next phase of Maia's transfiguration into a human form.

It was the dawn of the Winter Solstice. As humanity gathered around the globe to ask that more light come to the earth, waiting for the sun to rise and give the sign that Helios had once more returned to bask the Earth in his Light, the Immortals gathered to use that energy to create one of their own.

They came together at the meeting place walking through the portal, as if from thin air, into the circle of stones that held the energy of the work they were here to do. There would be a birthing on this day. The Immortals, known as the gods and goddesses of

Olympus and the Pantheon, were here to bring forth another one of their kind.

Athena came through the portal carrying the Palladium. It was their most sacred object, as it contained the essence of one of the original beings who had visited the Earth Plane long ago, and who had started the process of evolving the creatures of the planet into a higher consciousness. Athena was its guardian, the protector of its purity.

The stone circle had been prepared. There were lines of light connecting each stone, one to the other and then circles within circles within circles. Athena carefully placed the Palladium at the exact center of the circles. Each Immortal present went up to the Palladium and touched it silently for a blessing in preparation for the work they were there to do. Then each one went to take their place within the interlocking circles. The Palladium pulsed with creation energy. Atlas and Pleione stood on either side of it with their hands clasped, enfolding the Palladium in a circle of their arms. They were surrounded by a circle of male Immortals.

Male Immortals: the manifestation energy of that circle crackled in the air around them. The oneness of the Divine Masculine manifested into the duality of the Earth Plane as the physical representation of the *Doing Energy* of Source. Two other circles of female Immortals interlocked with the masculine circle. The female Immortals held the *Energy of Creation* and provided the creation matrix to generate the manifestation of the masculine circle.

Each circle joined hands and Atlas began the work with a single, deep throated note that was picked up by the rest of the Gods. The droning chant went up two notes and then slid back down. Went up again and held. Pleione joined in and then the Goddesses high voices joined in the chant.

How to describe the sound of creation? Each voice held the notes in the perfection of the God or Goddess as they were manifested. The deep timbre of the male voices was buoyed up by the lighter tones of the feminine. As the tones of the inner and outer circles merged, another layer of sound was added to the chanting. It was as if the angels sang with them. The sound of creation? Simple, clear notes that held the fullness and wholeness of existence itself. As the tones changed higher and lower, the light within the circles was blinding to mortal eyes.

Atlas and Pleione became pillars of Light. Rays of light radiated out from each pillar and twined around the Palladium in the double helix structure of DNA. Their essence merged and a bright beam of light shot up into the heavens and down into the earth.

***

Maia breathed her first breath. *I FOCUS. I FEEL. I AM.* Maia was at the point of revelation in form. Maia pulsed as her heart beat in rhythm to the earth. Maia burned with the life force within her. Maia reached and had hands that did the reaching.

Maia stepped forth and bent down to Atlas and Plieone. She gently touched them on the brow and they were immediately refreshed from their labor of creation. A breeze of fresh air blew through the circle as everyone felt the presence of the Divine touch them as a consequence of their labor of this day. For a moment they almost lost their form in their closeness to Source, but the song of a nearby bird pulled them back into the here and now.

The presence of "Will To Be" in its feminine form permeated the circle. Just for a minute the Lord of Will To Be held the circle in his regard. The gods and goddesses who had gathered for this ritual birthing became beams of shimmering light. The circle seemed to float away into another dimension just for an instant. Then they were back in their human form. Tears were in the eyes of all present. Time was such that days passed while they caught up to where they actually were in time and space. Each god and goddess bowed down to Maia and welcomed her to Earth. It was time for her to begin her work upon the Earth Plane.

Maia called upon Form to wrap itself around her and a robe of the softest silk appeared upon her body. The elementals swarmed around her waiting for her command. The gods and goddesses waited upon her command to do her bidding within the Earth Realm.

Maia felt the power of the physical form flow through her and the tug of the ocean as it flowed through her veins. She looked through time and saw the many patterns of energy that were hers to follow. There was one student in the distant future who needed her help in understanding the magic and the teachings that she was here to give. It was a strange connection that one so distant could be so present. She turned her attention to the future as form understood it and sent out a part of herself through time to anchor the connection. If the teachings were to be lost or distorted here in her now, then perhaps they could reemerge at a later date when humanity would better be able to use them.

***

I am floating above the earth. I am a part of the earth. I put it on like a mantle. My consciousness expands until I am a part of everything and…and… what is that noise?

I awaken. Who am I? What am I? The alarm! I automatically turn it off and in so doing I become aware of my body. My body … it hurts to shift back into the awareness of my body. My neck hurts from the way I was laying. I have to go to the bathroom. Like now. I am still out of it as I stumble across the room and into the bathroom. I hardly register what I am doing as I recall my dreams. To be a Goddess birthed in Light. What an experience! I can still feel the waves of energy; feel the power of the ritual calling forth a form to fit Maia.

I come back to bed and start to write everything down, at least as much as I have words for. It feels like I am split in two. That part of me that floats in the dream energy is ecstatic and joyous and whole. The part of me in the here and now is aching and sore and feels wounded. I feel so small and at the same time so big. It's hard to explain the dichotomy of my experience. I finally give up and go down to make my morning tea. Lots of cream and sugar this morning. And lots of caffeine. I need to clear out my brain to face my day.

***

A couple of days have gone by since the incredible dreams of birthing Maia. I was euphoric all day after the dreams. Now I feel cranky and I ache emotionally and physically. My dreams are nondescript. There are no voices in my head. I feel awful. I can't figure out what is wrong with me. I have a quiet weekend ahead of me starting tomorrow. Perhaps I can get rested up.

It's Saturday morning and I am sitting in my back room sipping tea, soothing ginger jasmine. I slept in this morning and I still feel like I haven't slept in days. I think about Maia and my dreams. The magnitude of my experience seems to dwarf my everyday life. It still hurts. I feel so let down. I guess that was it for my dreams and the hooded one. Still, it was an incredible experience. If only I knew what to do with it.

"I could help."

She's here in my head. I mean I hear her voice. I mean yes. Yes, I would like some help.

"Think about how you feel for a few moments."

I focus on my body and its aches and pains. My heart feels like it has been broken and my brain is foggy. I yearn to be reconnected to that vastness, yet I am afraid to feel all that grandeur and joy, and then feel small again.

"It's like you were a puddle of water and then experienced what it is like to be the ocean."

Yes, but now I am the puddle again, and I don't like it.

"You are a puddle who has the memory of being an ocean and all of a sudden being the puddle is too limiting."

Yes, exactly. How do I get beyond this?

"The transition will become easier with time and experience. I am sorry. I did not realize that the backlash of energy would be so great."

So this is backlash from what I experienced? That sort of makes sense, but how do I get over it?

"Be patient. You will feel better. Are you willing to try something with me?"

I hesitate. The Hooded One's ideas of what would make me feel better might be very different from my own.

"For just a minute, focus on being a puddle."

I think about puddles and feel my edges, not too far away, not very deep and I'm a little murky.

"Now think about being the ocean."

I immediately expand. I am vast waters that are deep and flowing. I have boundless life within me. I have shores that define my shape. Wait. Shores. Edges. I'm just a very big puddle.

Now think about being a drop of water."

Okay. I'm a drip. I mean a drop. (She doesn't laugh. Oh, well.) I am water. I am water that flows and evaporates and freezes. I am an ocean. I am a cloud that blows through the heavens. I am a glacier that moves slowly over the earth. I am viscous-like the sap in a tree. I am the blood in my veins. I like being water.

"So be the water in the puddle and you will feel better."

Hmmm. The Hooded One is right. I do feel better.

"Get us another cup of tea while you think."

So she likes tea. Maybe she is okay after all. What will our next adventure be? There is no answer in my head but I feel drawn to know.

Chapter Two

"Well, Form does not do so well when it's not connected to its soul."
The Hooded One

I have been hoping to dream with The Hooded One for a couple of days now, but my dreams have been the mundane variety all week. About as mundane as the dishes I am doing now. I think about The Hooded One and pause. The soapy water is dripping off my hands and my gaze is penetrating the wall in front of me as I see the hooded figure. The Hooded One. My mind has turned it into a name. How odd.

What had she called me? Igna…no, Ignomatius. I dry my hands and leave the dishes for later. I google Ignomatius and nothing comes up. The book of Greek legends is lying on my computer desk. If I can't find anything on my name, then I'll look up Maia's name.

Maia was the eldest of seven sisters who, as a group, were called the Pleiades. I am familiar with the Pleiades from star gazing. Each sister had a story passed down through the ages. Maia lived in a cave and had a son, Hermes, with Zeus. That was about it for information about Maia. I put the book down in frustration again as the images from my dream filled in the one dimensional lines with a vibrant, powerful woman whom all the gods and goddesses bowed down to. The legend in the book seemed like a minor tale of the eldest of the Pleiades, but my experience of her was of a vast, powerful energy taking form as a human.

I could still feel the depth and mystique of her presence, like the profound beauty of a sunset on a lake as the lush plant life breathed promised meaning, and the reflected colors of the sun on water painted the world with muted mystery. I sat motionless in front of the computer, lost in the wonder of my thoughts of Maia until it was time for bed.

                                    ***

I am following The Hooded One down the steps. At last, I am dreaming with her again. I hesitate from placing my foot on the next step as thoughts of Maia run through my mind. The Hooded One turns toward me and pauses. My questions jumble up around my tongue. What are we doing? Why Maia? Why are you calling me Ignomatius? My name is …. The Hooded One raises her hand and my thoughts stop.

"Your name is not important. Your soul is what I am here to connect with. It is your soul that has called out to the universe. Calling you Ignomatius takes you out of your everyday self and gives you a new identity beyond your physical world."

But surely you can tell me your name.

"Ignomatius, there are vast mysterious energies that move through the cosmos. Tiny parts of them connect into the world you know. Your species likes to name them as if a name can embrace the mystery of the beyond in a few letters that try to contain meaning. I will not be defined by your naming. Accept mystery and the unknown as a friend. Let a wisp of power beyond imagination be your guide."

But where are you guiding me to?

"Your histories, as you have read in the few lines of the legends around the Pleiades, are woefully lacking in the authentic meaning of what truly happened. You asked for spiritual adventure. Well, take a new look at an old story and see beyond the trite passages handed down through time to the living beings who came to your planet to create change."

As she speaks, her arm starts to rise. Am I going back to Maia again?

"There were seven sisters, Ignomatius. Maia was but one. Electra is your journey point tonight."

As she speaks the light gathers at the end of her finger tips. I am pulled into the vortex, a spiraling light that strips me of all physical sensation and thought.

                                    ***

I am walking along a path that parallels a large body of water. The cobalt blue of the water catches my eye. I walk through the shade of old pine trees that have battled the winds of the oceans for all their lives. Ah, I recognize where I am now from my travels through Europe. I am standing on the shore of the Mediterranean Sea.

The twisted trees on the shore frame a figure walking before me on a sandy beach. Could it be Electra? Her slight form should be buffeted by the winds but the winds part around her. I hurry to get closer. As I approach, I feel a shift in perception. My eyes no longer see the figure walking before me. I am looking through Electra's eyes.

***

Electra walked along the beach breathing in the fresh air. Although the warmth of the noonday sun enveloped her face and shoulders, she shuddered. Her vision of the future weighed heavily upon her heart, like the gathering of a brooding storm. The soft ocean breezes kissed her raven-black hair, yet she was oblivious to their sensual allure. Her attention was turned inward where a terrifying vision sliced across the timeline of the world.

A great darkness covered humanity's connection to All That Is. Humanity would flounder in separation for centuries, not sure of the existence of God or Goddess. Surely there must be a way to avoid such exile and pain. She stopped and stared out at the sea, but her eyes did not really see what lay before her. Instead she saw fouled waters and air not fit to breathe, winds carrying horrid smells much worse than the stench of carrion. She saw hordes of starving humans and animals, and vast areas of wastelands where there should be abundance and overflowing life. What frightened her the most was the legacy of bloodshed that stained the coming centuries: the needless deaths in numbers great and small, all committed in the name of God. The depth of the abyss created in human consciousness when their connection to Source was obliterated by Darkness sent a chill through her form that even her direct expression of love in form could not warm. So this was what fear felt like. It did not feel good.

As one of the Immortals, she knew on every level of her being that there was a plan for the glorious experiment of Source creating the Earth Plane and experiencing Itself as Form. A plan that directed the energy down to the slowest vibration of existence and back to the highest expression of All That Is. Still, every level of her being rebelled at the vision of that plan as it lay before her; sometimes having the Sight was as much a curse as it was a gift.

Surely this path had been revealed to her so she could do something to change it. Even the Weaver, who fabricated all of time and circumstance, made changes. Of all the Pleiadian sisters, Electra was the most powerful and Source must want her to intervene on Its behalf. Why else would she have received this vision? It would be better to change the timeline now before the Darkness descended upon the Earth rather than wait until the Plan was in full swing.

Changing the Plan would require a huge energy transformation and could not be enacted without the help of another powerful Immortal -- someone powerful, yet easily persuaded to intervene. Some of her sisters held back their power just because they thought they should not interfere in the Plan. She knew that the Plan was dynamic and adapted to choices made in a moment of Freewill. Her freewill propelled her to vanquish the probable future of pain and destruction for the beautiful earth and her children and she had a strategy that would impose **her** choice of light over darkness.

***

I shift out of Electra's vision and I am disoriented for a few moments. My sense of smell tells me I am in a musty, earthy place but my eyes are not adjusted to the dim environment before me. I seem to be in a cave and I can hear someone muttering in the background. As my eyes adjust, I look around and see an extraordinarily handsome man; no, make that a god in a corner of the cave. His energy signature is off the charts and lights up the area around him. Suddenly I can hear his thoughts. It's Zeus!

Zeus was in hiding. Well, he wasn't exactly hiding. He just didn't want to be bothered by anyone while he was doing his work. Well, it wasn't exactly work, it was really art, but Hera and Athena had called it craft the last time they had caught him doing his art, and he certainly didn't need to have them criticizing his art work. What did they know about art anyway? Sparks of divine thought ricocheted off the walls and ceiling of the cave. He refocused on his work; he didn't want to melt it just because he wasn't paying attention. He had learned to hone his wild lightning into a really fine light that he wielded to sculpt stone. It gave him a lot of pleasure to work with the stone and use his fire energy in a creative manner. Well, he got to create out in the world, but it was different than this. Mostly, he just smote things and people because they were so annoying, always petitioning for this or that. What did he care? He was here for the women anyway. Or they were here for him. He could never decide which way it worked. All the goddesses liked using him for sex magic because he was so powerful. Hera just didn't seem to understand his purpose. She was always nagging him to settle down. His fire was to stimulate life force on this planet and what better way to stimulate life force energy than to do sex magic? Leto had understood when they created Apollo and Artemis. Now that was some good sex magic.

His laser-like light was melting the stone. He had lost his focus again and would have to start over. It happened every time he started thinking about Hera or about sex magic. Focus. He examined the stone in front of him; his specialty was making miniature statues of the goddesses he had slept with in exact detail. There were several likenesses of Hera on the shelves in the cave. Some were her in ecstasy and some were her in anger; most of the time he couldn't tell the difference.

He didn't tell the goddesses that he took a little of their essence during sex to use in his art. He used it to create the finer details and imbue each statue with their life force. Feminine energy carried the divine spark of life force. He needed it for his art and if he had to take it without permission, then so be it. He was Zeus and he shouldn't have to ask permission. His method created magnificent likenesses, if he said so himself, and he had to, since he couldn't let anyone see what he had created. It was just as well. Here he could relax and just be himself, with no one bothering him to do this or that.

Zeus focused on creating the line of Hera's jaw with its bold angle that expressed her feminine strength. Then he carved the arch of her eyebrows that could express an open invitation or indignation depending on the light in her eyes. Her eyes…they held so much light. Eyes that…wait, someone was seeking him. He felt eyes looking for him. It would be best to go to a place where he could be found rather than have someone show up in his secret place.

****

Electra had been preparing for this day for many weeks. She had meditated on her vision for several days and identified the timelines that needed to be changed. She had done a cleansing fast for seven days, so that her form would be at its optimum for this kind of ritual. She had chosen Zeus even though she had not worked with him before, and from what the other goddesses said, he was the least likely to question anything to do with sex magic. Besides, he was one of the most powerful gods energetically and she wanted someone who could be easily led into her plan and still have the power to aid her in the work.

Electra was an air goddess. She worked with air elementals and on the mental plane. She helped fashion the mind of man, teaching discipline and focus. She was the embodiment of Intent in Form. Her intent at the moment was to fashion Form to fully hold this Intent: to bring Darkness into Light, to be the highest and best expression of Love in form and to have Form be an expression of the Love as a direct expression of All That Is on the Earth Plane.

She went over her vision of the ritual one more time before she called upon Zeus. First, she saw the threads of her original vision of the future. She watched as each thread led into the Darkness from which emerged Light. She gently touched those threads in her mind and felt their essence. In the back of her awareness, she could feel the Weaver as she wove together the threads of time and space and thought. She did not want the Weaver to be aware of her plan, so she very carefully marked the threads for change. "Threads" was such an odd word to describe the essence of the timelines and the weaving of Light into time and space.

It never occurred to her that she shouldn't alter the timelines. She was after all, Electra, a being of power and a direct expression of Source upon the Earth. She would not have been given the gift of Seeing the timelines if she was not permitted to change them. Why should she include her sisters in her plans? They did not have her vision or her gift. She knew what was right and would act to make it so. Surely that was the real reason Source had created her, as its divine expression upon this Plane, to do what the others either could not see or would not do. This was part of the Plan, and she was the divine instrument of the moment. And so was Zeus, whether he knew it or not.

She held Zeus in her conscious thought and called him to her. The Immortals did not actually have to travel to change location, they only had to be in the moment and hold that moment in their being. Thinking of Zeus would bring them together in space and time. As she felt him approach, she raised her right hand straight up so the palm faced outward, which was the signal to initiate sex magic among the Immortals. She wanted to engage Zeus in the energy even before he had time to think about what was happening, to be sure he would respond impulsively so that she didn't have to fully explain her plan to him.

***

Zeus saw Electra facing him with her right hand up in the air and palm forward. His physical form responded immediately. Electra! He had never performed sex magic with her. She would be a great addition to his collection. He tucked that thought into a dark corner of his mind. The Immortals were telepathic and had access to All Knowing. They had learned a few tricks in Form that were not openly discussed, like hiding a thought in shadow so it wouldn't be visible to those around. It seemed convenient in a world where Form had slowed to its lowest vibration. Some thoughts were best left unshared. The Immortals had learned not to probe too deeply in the mind's shadows. Open hearts could be damaged by what was found there. Even the thought of a heart being damaged was a product of the slow vibration of Form. Zeus turned his attention back to Electra. She stepped closer and blew her breath up his arm. The hairs stood up and it felt as though an electric shock went through him. The wonders of physical experience!

"Electra, how may I be of service?"

"Zeus, I need your help. Only you are powerful enough to do this work with me."

Sparks flew out around him as Zeus flaunted his power. It seemed to enthrall her so he blew a breath onto her neck. Her energy responded by encircling the two of them. "What did you want to do this day?"

Electra had carefully thought out how to present this to Zeus. On the one hand, she didn't want him to know exactly what she had planned, but on the other, she needed his full consent to use his energy for the working. "As you know I am a Seer. There are certain timelines where The Weaver has directed my attention that need modified for the highest good of all. I need your help with this working."

Zeus was taken aback. The Weaver didn't normally allow anyone to change the timelines. They were held in her hands and her hands alone. "I don't recall The Weaver letting anyone adjust the timelines. Are you sure?"

"I have been honored to be selected as a student of The Weaver because of my ability to See the timelines so well. This is one of Her assignments to me. I assure you, we will only work on timelines that are beneath Her notice. She has so much to keep track of as She weaves the Light. I am honored to be selected to help."

Zeus watched her closely. He noted the shadows within shadows of her thoughts. He lightly reached out to touch the shadows to see what was there. Electra reacted immediately. "Why are you probing my thoughts?"

"It is such an unusual request and I could not see the signature of The Weaver in your energy."

"The ways of The Weaver remain hidden to even the Immortals. I am not allowed to share the process, not even with you, oh mightiest Zeus." Electra breathed on his ear. His body shuddered in response.

Surely, this was a true recognition of his power that even The Weaver needed his participation in Her work. "I will gladly help you with your ….assignment."

Electra smiled and the world lit up around them. "First we must cast a circle around us, for this is most holy work." She needed their energy isolated from the others on Mt. Olympus so no one would suspect the nature of what she was doing and try to interfere. Zeus waved his hand and a pillar of light appeared at the cardinal points around them. He waved his hand again and the pillars expanded to envelop them in a bubble of light. He glowed and for a moment Electra saw why he was considered the most powerful of the masculine Immortals.

They stepped closer until their lips nearly met, breathing in and out together. Each breath aligned their energy for the work. Each breath energized their systems and their connection. Electra started to chant while she visualized the timelines that needed to be shifted. With his deep voice blending perfectly with hers, Zeus joined in as soon as he perceived the rhythm. Her visualization was so enhanced by his power that the timelines started to appear around them, dancing in and out of focus. They both stood entranced as they chanted with their breath in perfect harmony.

When she felt the timing was right, she switched her breathing pattern to alternate with his, so that the circuit of sexual energy would flow one to the other. Again, the power increased. They were both feeling the power, and focused on the chant to maintain their connection. Electra stretched out her hand and touched Zeus's heart and nearly fainted with the power flowing in the circle. She reached out to the timelines around them and started manipulating the weave, so that the Darkness would be gone forever.

Zeus pulsed with energy as Electra's hand on his heart connected him to the timelines in her other hand. His mind raced as the shadows surrounding their work dispersed and the full scope of Electra's plan became revealed. This was not a minor weaving. This was a major reworking of the Light, and nowhere was the hand of The Weaver on the hand of Electra. This was the height of arrogance on her part, from the view of an Immortal who thrived on arrogance. It was too late to stop the working now. He could only give it all he had or else the fallout would affect all of time. Zeus placed his hands on the seat of Electra's genitals and the power exploded through them and the timelines. More and more power. Electra stared deeply into his eyes and in that moment they were so joined that even The Weaver could not have separated their Light.

Electra held fast to her vision of where the timelines should go to dispel the Darkness forever. The energy poured through her into the light around them, but it was not enough to shift the lines. She drew on Zeus. She needed more and more. She was so lost in her vision of change that she didn't notice that Zeus was going into a state of shock.

Zeus realized that it required too much energy to shift the timelines, even for him. His body started to convulse. He lost his voice and his focus. He was disappearing into the Light, never to return again. It was too much! He had only one thought left, "Break the contact," and mercifully, as his body convulsed, he was pulled away from Electra. He fell to the ground, writhing in pain and moaning so deeply that even the rocks beneath him echoed the sound.

Electra reeled with the onslaught of energy around her that was so unbalanced now that her connection with Zeus was broken. The work must be finished. The Darkness must be dispelled. She held her resolve and wrapped the energy patterns around her into the deepest core of her being. Other Immortals were approaching, brought running by Zeus's cries and convulsions. She stepped back as Hera and Athena raced to Zeus's side.

"What happened here?" Hera looked at her briefly and then back to her beloved Zeus.

"I don't know. He accosted me to do sex magic and when I refused he went into this fit!" Electra managed to twist the truth just enough to avoid drawing their attention back to her. No one doubted her.

"Athena, help me ground his energy. I have never seen him like this." Hera and Athena focused on Zeus.

Electra realized that she needed to find another way to finish the work. She had seen this possibility in the timelines, but it was very risky. Still, the whole world depended on her now and as luck would have it, Athena was one of the ones drawn to Zeus at this moment. Athena, guardian of the Palladium, the most sacred of all artifacts of the Immortals, was focusing on Zeus just as Electra would need the energy of the Palladium to complete her work. If Zeus could not generate the power that was needed, then surely the Palladium, that which contained the essence of one of the original Seven, would hold the energy needed for this great deed.

She silently slipped away from Athena and Hera and ran to the sacred site. She was nearly bursting with the energy that flowed through her from the disrupted working. She stood before the artifact in awe and wonder as her augmented sight connected with the Palladium's depth and power. She slowed her breathing and focused on her work once again. The timelines sprang up around her, spinning dizzily around and around, making it hard to focus. She called upon the energy and sacredness of the Palladium and drew in energy as it responded to her need. Surely this was meant to be and she was the instrument of Source. Time would be changed and the Darkness dispelled. Her focus became crisp and clear. She knew that she needed to merge with the essence of the Palladium to finish her work. She stepped forward and wrapped herself around the Palladium, an act forbidden to all but the most pure. As her body touched the artifact, a great stillness surrounded her and she was standing on a gray plain. She felt the eyes of The Weaver upon her and The Weaver's voice reverberated through her head.

"What are you doing my Child of the Light? No hands may touch the timelines but my own. No one may make use of the Palladium without my consent. It is your own arrogance that fuels this work, not the pure light of love. You do not trust in The Plan. Your Light is tarnished in this contact. Be gone!"

As the Palladium was torn from her grasp, Electra felt as if the very core of her being was splintering. Her connection to the timelines around her vanished and she stood outside of time. Or was it *in* the essence of time? Her thoughts spun within her head until thoughts held no meaning. Her sense of self unraveled from its anchor to her foundation. The light was being drained from her essence so fast that she could not maintain her identity. And then there was only Darkness, the Darkness that she so desperately wanted to banish for all eternity.

***

And then there was only Darkness. Are my eyes opened or closed? Who am I? What is this Darkness all around me?

"Breathe, Ignomatius! Breathe deeply."

Her voice in my head telling me to breathe. Whose voice? Her voice. I breathe. My body shudders. My body!! I breathe again. Still darkness.

"Open your eyes, dear one."

Her voice. Where are my eyes? Aren't they open? All I can see is darkness.

"Breathe through your nose. Breathe through your eyes. Feel your eyelids. Flutter them. Flutter your eyelids for me."

I never flutter my eyes! Upon her command, my eyes open, just like that. Oh! I see light, early morning light. I'm back. Her laughter peals through my head. Is that relief I sense?

"Oh it is relief, my dear one. I see that your travels in the past are going to be way too adventuresome. How did you get to Electra's downfall so quickly? I must admit I wasn't quite ready for us to go there."

You weren't ready? How did I get there? How did I get back here!

"Breathe some more. How about a nice cup of tea?"

I realize that I hurt all over and my brain is so foggy I can hardly think. I need a trip to Starbucks for a caramel macchiato.

"Coffee makes it harder to connect, Little One."

Good. Then I will have two or three. I feel The Hooded One recede. I slowly get out of bed. Did I say that everything hurts? I'm trying not to think. I need coffee, perhaps, I'll have a double shot in that caramel macchiato.

***

It's been a couple of days since I witnessed the downfall of Electra. I didn't just witness it. I felt like I was there with her. I'm just starting to recover. This has felt like the aftermath of a bad flu. I can't seem to clear my head and I can hardly move. I had to call off work. Who would believe me that I called off work because of the witnessing of the sex magic of a god and goddess through a dream? How can I believe it? I've never even tried sex magic. Sex is never going to be the same after that experience. I sip my lemon zinger tea and mull over the whole Zeus/Electra experience. I don't know whether to laugh or cry, feel exalted or languish in the depths of despair, savor the rush of sexual rapture or be crushed by the brick wall of Darkness. Mostly, I just want to sleep. Thank goodness, it is sleep and only sleep.

***

I am standing on a gray plain. There is nothing around me. I am surrounded by a flat, gray landscape. It seems familiar somehow. Something about the grayness. A shock goes through me. Electra! Electra was standing on a gray plain just before The Weaver smote her from existence.

"Goddesses cannot be smote from existence."

This is a different voice in my head. It is not The Hooded One's voice.

"No, it's not. And you were not meant to be woven into the 'Zeus/Electra experience'. I am here to reweave that which was not meant to be in the pattern."

I feel a gentle touch. A healing touch. I sink back into unawareness. I realize that I feel better even as I float away. I see stars, a million stars and lines of light everywhere. There is a tangle in the lines like a knot. I feel her again, the one who healed me. She is studying the knot. I watch her hands touch the tangle and gently tease away some of the frayed lines of light. Is that a sigh I hear?

"I am The Weaver, but some knots can only be untangled by their maker. This one will have to wait until it can be rewoven into the Plan."

I drift away filled with wonder and awe. What have I witnessed this time?

***

I open my eyes again. I remember weird dreams again. Light and hands and more light. Oh, I feel good this morning. I actually feel human again. I think I am going to live. That weaving stuff just might be okay after all.

"Good morning."

Her voice is in my head, and a welcome voice it is. Good morning to you. I see her step back and take a long look at me. Her eyes study me like she's never seen me before.

"You have the signature of The Weaver on you."

Is that who that was? The weaver who weaves all of life together? Cool.

"Cool indeed. This is interesting. Very interesting. It seems that our work has attracted the attention of The Weaver. I am not sure if that is good or bad."

Well, I certainly feel better for it.

"I must admit that I am relieved that you are doing better. Your energy patterns were not good after that last journey. I didn't want to say anything at the time, but you almost went into the Darkness with Electra."

And if I had gone into the Darkness with Electra.....

"Well, Form does not do so well when it's not connected to its soul."

You mean like it dies or something?

"Well, something."

I sit soberly for a few minutes while I ponder the implications of this. I could die from one of these dreams.

"Oh, Ignomatius, that is part of why I am here. I not only guide, but I protect you as well. You are safely held in my light. We will talk more about this later."

I hope that my idea of being safely held in her light, and her idea of safely holding me are one and the same. And what about that bit of "part of why I am here." What's the other part anyway? Of course, she's not around to answer that question right now. I'll have to file it away under "Make sure to get this answered soon." Unfortunately, that file is starting to get thick.

***

I am following the Hooded One down the steps. Down and down to the place where we do our work. I am not sure if I am ready for this. My experience with Electra took too much out of me. I know the Hooded One will protect me, but from what?

"Do not worry, Little One. What I have in mind for tonight is quite different from the connection where you experience the lives of the Seven Sisters. Trust me and follow."

I am still surprised when she first reads my thoughts. I keep following her down the steps knowing that she can feel the trepidation in my heart. We get to the room at the bottom. It's different this time.

"Or has it always been this way and you simply did not see?"

I do not answer her question as I look around. There is a fire place with a fire burning in the corner with a table nestled in between two overstuffed chairs. It looks . . . cozy. Again I am surprised.

"You have experienced the birth of a goddess and witnessed a desecration of the most sacred artifact of all time. Yet you are still surprised by what you see here. I love the human mind."

I muffle my mental response to her gentle teasing. So what are we going to do? She walks to one of the chairs, sits, and then gestures for me to sit also. I am tentative as I take my place opposite her. I feel her mental reassurance wrap around me like a down-filled blanket on a chilly evening.

"Try to relax, Ignomatius. Here is what I would like to try tonight. Your last journey with Electra was much too taxing on your energy. And, quite frankly, the experience has set off your psychic security alarms. I think it would help your connection to take some time and energy to become more familiar with the Seven Sisters."

I am skeptical, but continue to listen closely as she speaks.

"I think that it would be helpful if you could hear their thoughts and feel their energy to strengthen the bonds. It will make for smoother transitions on your part. Their story is not without trauma and excitement.

32

I do not want to lose our connection because the trauma overshadows the work."

Do I truly have a choice about this connection? She looks deeply into my eyes for a moment. I cannot see her face because of the hood, but I feel the searching look. There is a sense of sadness in her concern.

"There is always a choice in this reality, which is part of the joy and part of the curse even for the Immortal Beings. You can choose not to participate in this work. Do you want to continue, Little One?"

How do I explain the impact of that simple question? It is like doors that had been closed all my life opened up and let light shine through into dusty, unused corridors of my mind. Even her use of the term "Little One" rather than Ignomatius created rays of Light through my whole being. I knew in this moment I faced a decision that would change my life irrevocably. Did I want to continue? I know with all my being there is only one answer to that question, no matter what the consequences are. Yes, I want to continue. I feel her sigh of relief as though there are hundreds watching this moment and hoping for the right outcome.

"Thank you for that choice, my friend."

Chills reverberate through my body as she speaks.

"Here is what I would like us to try. I am going to place my hands on your ears. Then we'll see what happens as you connect to the voices of the Seven Sisters."

I nod and watch the empty space of the hood as her hands move toward my head. It would be a comfort to have a face to connect to that voice.

"Not yet, Ignomatius. Not yet."

Her words echo on and on in my head even as her hands touch my ears. I am thrown into a world of light. The light melts the scene around me as I morph into thought without form. Her voice fades away, and I hear a voice, someone that I have longed to hear and then another and another.

***

"First is Maia!"

"We have touched minds before, you and I, little one who wishes to dance with the stars. For that is what we do in the heavens, dance with the stars until the Darkness is lifted from the minds of men.

"Do you have sunrise where you can see it in the morning there? I loved to watch sunrise. To see the great orb of light emerge over the horizon and light up my mountain rock by rock and bush by bush. I would gather in that freshness every day and renew myself in Form. The very life force around me would sing its greeting to the Sun and the Sun would sing back in all its glory.

"There is such fundamental power in your world. Life touching life. Life moving from place to place. Life growing in such unlikely places. It always astounded me. Such gifts to the Goddess exist there. I am always grateful to be a part of it, even when my Immortal heart breaks over some misdeed of Man.

"Invoke the elements around you and feel our magic that thrives in those elements still. Heed our voices in the life around you, for the echoes of our joy linger still within the cycles of life and death."

"Next is Taygeta."

"West is the direction of the setting sun. I seldom turned my attention to that side of the work. I was so involved in the new beginnings and in the grounding of inherent knowledge that we brought to the Earth Plane. The Sacred Circle was complete within us and I thought that I need not concern myself with the completion of our task, which would just come on its own from the power of the magic that we performed with our work. I should have known better. Ah-h, the 'shoulds' have always been one of the banes of physical existence. Each one of us needed to be complete within her work in order for the circle to be complete.

"So we wait for the circle to come to completion. Thank the Goddess, we get to wait in the Light rather than endure the centuries and the Darkness in flesh. As dearly as I loved being in flesh, it was ever so easy to shed when we returned to the Light.

"Now you call us with your slow thoughts and resistant heart to bear the noise and confusion of life on Earth again. It is so quiet in the Light. There is the eternal singing of joy, but it is like a heartbeat. It pulses through all Being, and most times remains just below the threshold of awareness.

"There I go again, thinking that I do not need to pay attention to the details. Apparently I am not done with this lesson that started in flesh.

"How do you stand the pain of being mortal, Ignomatius? How do you stand the pain of separation? It is too much to contemplate while I still linger on the Plane of Light. Better that someone else bears the flesh and I only need communicate my story."

"Next is Merope."

"Lust flows through the body and expands our senses beyond the normal ken of activity. We were in a constant state of lust. Everything stimulated our senses and aroused our passion, which was perhaps the effect of being an immortal being in Form.

"That whole connection is so distant to you now. Immortal Beings become a legend, a fairy tale. Perhaps you will get to remember what it is to be immortal in flesh, to not be trapped by time and space. The limitations of time and space have left scars upon you, binding your spirit and flesh to the illusion of time and locking you away from the river of grace. The key to wholeness lies within you. Let the joy of oneness spread through you into every breath and deed. Unravel the hold illusion has upon you and the knowledge that you seek will become apparent through the transparent nature of time and space. It is as simple as a passing thought."

"Next is Sterope."

"Jealousy. Now, that is a human emotion that I am well familiar with. I was persistently jealous of my husband with his constant, unending adoration of our daughter. My other sisters all had husbands that would do anything for them. Oenomaus would only do things for Hippodamia.

Hippodamia… Hippodamia… Hippodamia. I loved my daughter. She took to the teachings like a duck to water while my son went off and got entangled with the Nymphs and totally forgot everything I taught him.

"It's not easy thinking of these things while being in the Light, you know. These kinds of thoughts do not translate well in the Light. It's hard to hold onto feelings and remember the importance of emotions, but jealousy I remember. It nearly twisted me off my path and caught us all by surprise. Jealousy is the well of insecurity that flows up and poisons the mind and the heart. Who would have thought it could be so powerful and so seductive?

"Our plan was to teach the mysteries to mortals. It was the most rewarding part, other than existence in Form itself. We fell so in love with experience and sensation and the beauty of the senses. Truly, Gaia created a marvel when she created herself as Form. Of course, we created disarray within that creation, just a vibrational change here and there. After all, we were Immortal Beings, our very vibrational nature wrought change in everything we touched."

"Next is Electra."

"The Immortal Beings were connoisseurs of life. We did not have parent issues or debilitating childhoods. We were arrogant to the ultimate degree and sadly, sometimes, omnipotence did not mean wise or compassionate.

"Quite shockingly, we did not always agree while we were in Form. We were not prepared for the consequences of our disagreements. In Light, they meant so little. We would inhabit a different portion of the spectrum. Most of the time, we could not even disagree in Light. It is beyond the vibrational nature of our beings.

"Yet in Form, the nature of our disharmony was very apparent, even to ourselves. It caught us completely unaware. How could we learn to negotiate our differences in Form and reestablish our harmony? We floundered in our divinity, and in so doing it generated serious consequences for humanity.

"Humans did not have all eternity to recuperate. In many cases, they did not recuperate at all. We spent their lives like coins bet on some cosmic game. It was unholy of us and in our *arrogance we did not recognize the enormity of our actions on those around us.*

"Mortals view time so differently; it is such a precious commodity to you. To us, it is an endless river. Humans do not perceive it so with their short, punctuated existence. Even though the soul continues on in time, the memory of that eternal connection gets lost in the translation of Light into Form. We could not comprehend the full effect of our behavior upon the human psyche, nor even begin to understand how they quested for what came so naturally to us. We spanned the centuries. It was not until we were denied entrance into Form that we began to understand what our presence on Earth had done to humanity. There are those who do not acknowledge it still."

"Next is Alcyone."

"Hold the course. Set your sight on the port and hold the course. I learned that from the sailors who crossed my waters as they carried my name upon their lips. Was I a master of air or water? It was the storm I could control from deep within the waters where I lived. How could Form live within water when it walked upon two legs? You assume, perhaps, too much. As you well know, the sisters were not human. We were divine thought and as such we manifested ourselves in the form that was appropriate for our task. What was our task? Ah-h...a much better question than what was our form.

"Our tasks lie within what you call the Mysteries, but we each held specific roles and duties within that task. Some of us fulfilled those duties better than others. Some of us were not so tempted by flesh that we lost sight of our reason for being.

"Do you know how many sailors I did not help just because I did not like their ship? Or maybe the wind was good for me, the way it was blowing. Saving humanity was never my goal. I did the prerequisite "save the sailors from the storm". Still, it was the Earth, herself, who held me enthralled. The

way she put together the building blocks of life. Her elemental energy was phenomenal. Superb. Now that held me to the course."

"Last is Celaeno."

"Light is such an interesting phenomenon in Form. Here it has substance and temperature and even odor. Who would have thought that Light could be divided from itself? That experience, alone, is worth the sojourn on Earth.

"While fire can consume earth, water can control fire. Air is an essential ingredient of them all, the main ingredient actually. Earth, in turn, transmutes all the other three. There is no dominance as humans tend to categorize things, only the interplay of elements exchanging and transforming within themselves and within each other.

"This is the power of the Earth spirit. To take such simple building blocks and create complex and intricate patterns of love. This is the intoxication of the Form that holds us captive to the flesh. To touch and feel and taste and smell, to transform and create infinitely. Human consciousness adds awareness with choice and the variables are astronomical within each moment, flowing one to the other and back again.

"It is a marvel and a wonder. It is small wonder that we pay such homage to the Goddess who is Form. Gaia. Earth. Terra. She holds the keys of life and love within her hands and plays them so masterfully upon us all."

***

The Weaver's hand hesitated ever so slightly as she chose the next strand of Light to weave together. This one was back on the path! Too much Light tended to overwhelm and too little left it starving and afraid. She peered into the strand in her hands to better see the one. There were shadows within the Light all around the one. Ah-h-h, fear was doing its job of hiding the Light here. Fear cast shadows within the Light so that those on the Path could not see. She wove a bit of Light into the shadows and then into the one. Then She added another strand that became a bright path into the next weave for the one. This was a path that even

the shadow of fear could not hide. She continued her weaving at Her normal pace. Light to Light to Light.

***

I awaken from a dream about hands playing with stars. I snuggle down in the covers and gently hold the memory of my dream and watch the stars moving in intricate patterns. I see the Pleiades constellation form, dissolve, and form again. Oh, last night they talked to me. Electra talked to me. I've been worried about her after the Weaver sent her off. She must be okay. I know it's silly to worry. She is a goddess and all, and centuries have passed. Still, the memory is fresh in my mind. I savor their voices as they whirl around in my mind so clearly. It feels like receiving a call from a long, lost friend. My eyes fill with tears. Already, I feel so enmeshed in their story. I feel like I am being woven into their story somehow, if only as the teller of their tale.

"Only?"

Ah, good morning*!*

"You seem to be doing quite well this morning."

Yes, I had good dreams.

"Dreams?"

Well, whatever you want to call it. I had assumed you were one of them. Are you?

"That will be revealed in time, Little One. My identity is not important at this point."

A name would be nice. I am tired of calling you The Hooded One.

"I've grown accustomed to 'The Hooded One'. It matters not what you call me, I hear you always."

And I've never been comfortable with the "always" part. Some thoughts should not be shared.

"I enjoy your human thoughts. They add flavor to the Light that I am. I assure you, I do not eavesdrop on your every thought. However, breakfast does seem to be surfacing quite strongly now."

And a cup of tea to start my day. Any preferences this morning?

"Earl Grey, hot."

You are eavesdropping! That's from Star Trek.

"Another interesting flavor added to my Light."

39

Chapter Three

"Death is an essential part of life, like breathing and sex."
The Hooded One

I am sitting with The Hooded One near the fireplace; she is staring at the flames. I can feel her power dancing like the flames, quiet and beautiful, radiating warmth that touches the heart. She turns to me and I face the blank space that hides her essence. Still it does not feel blank to be held within her presence.

"You honor me with your thoughts, Ignomatius. We so seldom have quiet time in our lives. It is good to share it with you."

There is a deep smile in my heart. I find that the more I spend time with The Hooded One, the less I express myself to her with words or actions. I am learning her state of being; it is a true gift.

"As we proceed with our exploration of the Seven Sisters, I would like to try a more active direction on my part. It will, perhaps, help you not to get caught up in the story to the point where you might be ....damaged."

Oh, I would definitely appreciate avoiding damage.

"As I have said before, the story of the Seven Sisters is not without trauma and excitement. The trick is to guide you through their mysteries without exposing you to energies that could blow out your circuits, to use the modern analogy."

I do hear words in my head when The Hooded One speaks but how do I convey the intimacy of her thoughts flowing into mine? When she speaks of trauma and excitement, my body responds as if I were in a state of trauma and excitement. When she speaks of exploring mysteries, my body trembles with anticipation.

"My words and thoughts prepare you for your journey. I learn from you even as I teach. It is a gift to us both, Little One."

Again, there is that sense of being held in loving arms or wrapped in a safe cocoon.

"I would like us to start exploring the relationship of Merope and Sisyphus. Time has told quite a different tale of what happened in the ages past. The true story is hidden deep within the fragments of symbolism that remain in your history.

"Sisyphus, who was married to Merope, held much understanding in his bones, perhaps too much for his own good. Merope loved him beyond words for his goodness and intellect, which was sometimes tempered by wisdom and sometimes not. She taught him the deepest mysteries and he could fathom them all. He knew the fate of mankind that was to follow and suffered for it. Perhaps his biggest fault was lack of patience, but then what human soul knows the patience of millenniums? Your short lives leave you bursting forth like spring flowers to create as quickly as possible and as much as possible before your bloom withers. Sisyphus's bloom was so bright to Merope. Unfortunately for him, it was like a blight to some of the other Immortals, one to be extinguished and forgotten.

"Tonight, you will journey with Sisyphus and Merope to experience their tale. I will follow your thoughts and reactions, and if I feel you are getting too involved, I will pull you out. Do you understand? Are you comfortable with this path?"

Well, I am certainly willing to give it a try.

"Good. We will begin."

She raises her arm and points. My gaze follows. Again, my very being is drawn into a light so bright that I am blinded.

***

He knew that this was the one he wanted. So beautiful and fair with gentleness that radiated out from her. Yet he could feel her power. Earth power, like the rocks as they sat for hundreds of years and thought their slow thoughts. Merope was not slow, but her thoughts seemed to span the ages. He started reciting the most ancient texts that he could think of and all of the poetry within his heart. He followed her around, talking incessantly, and never repeating a saga or verse for days. Somehow, he knew this would catch her attention.

***

Merope watched his deep, dark eyes as he followed her around, talking incessantly, a constant shadow to her now. How could one vessel hold so much and not burst? His potential boiled over like one of the mineral springs where she enjoyed a bath. Perhaps she would like to bathe in him also. Where did that thought come from? He was a mortal, but such an intriguing mortal. All the Immortals knew that to become attached to the ones with such short lives was an unspeakable torture. One could never give them even one more day of life than their vessel was capable of, and what a delectable vessel he was. His physique was exquisite in its healthiness. His intelligence burned in his eyes. His passion shone out around him like a great halo of light.

She shivered and then caught her breath. Sometimes Form brought with it unexpected moments of pleasure, like now, as she had a physical reaction to her thoughts. Oh joy, oh bliss. No wonder the Immortals found Form so seductive and inviting, even with its limitations. Experience became so focused right down to the smallest detail.

She drank in the smell of the man who followed her and felt the quivering answer of her own flesh in response. It was a smell that stimulated the senses quite unlike other smells, a musky, vibrant strength. Why did she respond so to his smell? She was not sure but she knew she would have to find out and live with the consequences, come what may. Here was one worth the risk. Besides, what better way to teach the mysteries to mortals than through the flesh they inhabited so tightly? Earth was her specialty, and here was a specimen of Earth that she wanted to experiment with on a personal basis. Touch to touch. Breath to breath. Her own form brightened like a star for a moment as she became lost in her experience of the passion flowing through her veins. The man following her fell down on his knees, overcome with the light that he beheld within the Goddess he loved.

***

I am back with The Hooded One. This is unusual. I always wake up from one of these experiences as if from a dream, instead of going back to the room deep underground with The Hooded One.

"We are experimenting here, Ignomatius. I wanted to see if I could call you out of the light. How do you feel?"

I feel fine. I am always stimulated after witnessing the passion of the Immortals.

"Their passion could be just as deadly a trap as their anger. It draws you into their energy until nothing else will satisfy the senses. It is good that you can withdraw from this experience and feel all right. You are getting much better at this process."

I am not sure how to respond to this. I guess it is good that I am handling this better, but I am still ambivalent about the whole thing. Why me?

"It has taken you a while to ask that question. The answer lies in lifetimes of experience. It will seem simple enough, but there are so many layers of inexpressible connections that the very simplicity of it will not satisfy the intellect."

She looks deeply at me for a moment. I go still like a rabbit before a fox. I am not sure I want her to see me in this manner. It is a level of vulnerability that I have not experienced before. It really does feel like she is about to devour me. She pulls back and I breathe again. I didn't even realize that I had stopped breathing.

"Sorry to startle you so. I was probing your energy through your entity connection."

My Entity?

"Words are inadequate anytime one speaks of spirit. What I say is the truth but can only be a half truth, because words cannot convey the fullness of the whole truth. Do you understand?"

I think I do. I quiver inside. It's like I stand on the brink of a discovery of a great treasure. My entity.

"On the one hand, spirit is. That's the end of the description."

I sense a half hidden smile.

"On the other hand, spirit is expressed in form in layers of hierarchy. Most people would think of what I am calling the Entity as God. The godness of the entity is expressed in different aspects that become other entities that are expressed in aspects. These are the aspects that you would call soul. Are you with me still?"

As she speaks, I am lost in a vision of the Entity that makes my travels back to the Seven Sisters look like a movie. How to describe this? As she says the Entity, there is a vision of a vast amoeba-like being forming legs that reach out into deep, dark space. The legs of energy glow and then branch out into other legs and more legs, each time growing smaller and more focused. I can sense a purpose and organization that is totally directed by the original Entity, like a general directing the troops; no, more like a mother guiding her children as each one grows into its own sense of self. It looks like this vast cosmic map that shows how everything is interconnected. As I watch it grow, one of the legs lights up brighter than the others and my attention is focused there. I can see lines and energies moving from that one until it is directly connected to me. Then I light up and connections flow out of me. They are all aspects of God. For one very brief instant, I am The All. Then it all collapses in upon itself and I am with The Hooded One once more. My breath shudders, like I have run up a steep hill and overexerted my body. I feel her watching me closely. Her hand reaches to me and tenderly brushes my cheek. A sense of calm washes through me, and my breathing steadies. My shaking ceases, but I will never be the same. The vision of the Entity flows through me, through the room, through The Hooded One and beyond. Again she reaches out to me and touches me in the center of my forehead.

"Close your inner eyes for now and rest. We will come back to our journeys after you have assimilated this experience."

Suddenly I feel like a child who has stayed up late for the party and can't stay awake any longer. Just one more minute. I don't want to miss anything. I stare at the lights all around me, but my eyes keep closing. I fall into a profound sleep.

***

I am sitting in my back room watching the morning birds and drinking an absolutely perfect cup of tea. After my experience last night my senses are so …enhanced. The feel of the soft cotton of my pajamas, the smell and taste of my tea, the early morning light through the trees. These experiences nearly take my breath away as I focus from one sensation to another, and then hold them all together at once, like the grand entrance of an adagio at the symphony. I am an amoeba branching out into my back yard….

"Ground yourself, Little One."

Oh, good morning. I am drunk on my senses. I am woven into every bit of life force in the Universe. I am ….

"Focus on your breath. Breathe for me, a nice deep breath. That's good. Another. Wiggle your toes. Now as you breathe, send your energy down into the earth through your feet. Deep into the earth. Breathe. Take a sip of your tea."

I am my breath. I am my toes. I am my tea. Wait. I am not tea. I drink tea. I am my breath. I breathe. I am grounded. I feel the weight of my body.

"Tell me what you learned last night. Did you find the answer to why you are on this journey?"

It's sort of like I'm a distant cousin visiting a lost branch of the family and discovering the family history.

"That's very good. You've got the connection perfectly."

I can see the half-truth of the words of it. It cannot be expressed in simple words. Expressed? Described? Captured?

"Keep working on grounding yourself today, Ignomatius. Go for a walk. Maybe make some root vegetable soup. Take out the trash. Enjoy the beauty of your soul as it is expressed in this world."

I feel her fade away. I watch the light and the shadows of the trees. All is goodness.

***

I am sitting with The Hooded One near the fireplace. I don't remember getting here. It feels like we have been talking for a while.

"It's taken your energy a while to gather itself. I feel you here now. Good. We have more work to do tonight. What do you know of Sisyphus?"

He was the one who cheated Death and was punished by having to roll a giant rock up a steep hill. Then it would roll back down and he would have to start all over again.

"Much of the saga has been lost through the ages. The story of Sisyphus holds keys to Source that have been totally misinterpreted over the centuries, but he did cheat Death for a while. It was one of the Mysteries that Merope taught him. She could deny him nothing."

Can you teach me to cheat death? I can feel she is disturbed for a moment after my question.

"Death is an essential part of life, like breathing and sex. You come into this plane to have the experience of death as much as the experience of life. Why would you want to cheat yourself of what is essential to your soul?"

Well, it was just a thought. I do need to ponder her comment about death, but I guess not now. We have work to do.

"Our work is totally wrapped in the experiences of life and death. It was not a silly question, only a misdirected desire. Merope and Sisyphus were a team of great magical workers on this plane. For all the stories saying

he was a mere mortal, his ability to absorb the teachings of Merope set up pathways for humanity that affect the Weaving still. Sisyphus and Merope changed the pathway of humanity as much as Electra by their work, and were just as dedicated to holding a path of Light through the Darkness. Their arrogance matched hers, as well, only it manifested itself a little less dramatically. Well, I could carry on about them all night. Let's send you off to experience it for yourself."

I feel her assess me. I am ready for this.

"You are ready. Each journey into the Light prepares you for more, opening doorways within you that will change your pathway out of Darkness and into the Light."

As she speaks, she is slowly raising her arm and my gaze follows. I could no more resist that pointing arm than I could resist my beating heart, which is pounding as I vanish into the Light.

***

Merope and Sisyphus are standing at opposite cardinal points of a circle of people. She is at the northern point, holding the energy of the Unknown. He is at the southern point, holding the fire and passion of the noon day sun. The circle today holds more strangers than the regulars they usually work with. Sisyphus always tells their guests about the circle and many of them want to try it out for themselves. Who would pass up the chance to do ritual with a goddess and her earthly consort? Sisyphus doesn't happen to mention that sometimes the physical form doesn't survive their work. The energy generated in their circles was so powerful sometimes that people could not hold it and died. It was getting around that he killed his guests but they had all volunteered to be a part of a working. Her beauty alone tempted men to brave waters deeper than they could swim, which Sisyphus knew well. He, himself, would follow Merope anywhere. It was his destiny and he tread the waters of the energy with all of his being. He always managed to survive and he thrived on their work together.

Sisyphus kept his focus on Merope across the circle. It was time to join their energies. Merope held the energy of the North because her form was Earth. His energy held Fire. They would merge. Fire could be extinguished by Earth, and, unless he embraced the energy completely, he could be extinguished as well.

Merope started singing the note that accelerated the energy. Every cell in his body responded to that note and his voice joined hers, adding a baritone vibration: Fire and Earth voicing their passion. Melicertes added his voice as Air from the east; Ino, his mother, added her voice from the west. The mother and son energy generated by them added a depth to the working. They were seeding a vibrational change into the planet to hold the Light down through the Ages of Darkness.

Sisyphus and Merope had seen the results of the Age of Darkness from their energy work. As great as his passion was for Merope, his passion for creating change in the fate of mankind on the Earth exceeded the depths of his love for Merope. That passion was used to ignite the energy of the seed of knowledge into the Earth, itself, that would reside there until such time as it could be reawakened. The very chemical composition of the Earth would be transfigured to hold aspects of Source that would be spread through the ley lines, once they were released.

Melicertes held the intellectual pattern of the knowledge being seeded and guided as the representation of Air. Merope directed the pattern and grounded it into the vessel of Earth. Earth held the key to the Unknown, the door to the mysteries. Ino flowed into the pattern with the adaptability of Water and built into the pattern the seeds of completion that were held in the West. Their voices merged and a beam of light appeared in the center and opened a gateway to the center of the Earth. A deep hole appeared in the center of the circle beneath the beam of light; this was where they tended to lose other circle members if they could not hold the energy. Sisyphus fed his passion into the energy of air and water to stabilize the forms holding that portion of the circle. Merope's voice soared through the Light and her arms were raised as if she was embracing the light. He felt her touch across the circle as an embrace. He was filled with the love of that embrace like a child held in the arms of its mother, only it was the Child and the Mother. His was the love of new creation as expressed in a child's innocent love for mother.

Merope's arms started lowering and the note changed. The energy of the circle gathered and focused as it was directed into the chasm straight toward the center of the Earth. They were feeding Light to Gaia as she was expressed in Form, vibration to vibration. He could feel the earth pulse, feel it engulf him as his energy entered into the heart of the earth. He pulsed with Gaia's pulse. He pulsed with Merope's pulse. The energy held. Melicertes and Ino were able to hold the vibration at this level. He became the fire at the heart of the earth. Here fire and earth resided in harmony. It was bliss beyond words.

***

They were eating after the ritual. Everyone was ravenous after the work, and food helped ground them after the intense merging of the day. Each bite still held the blissful essence of earth being consumed by fire. Sisyphus could feel the sensations of the others in the room as they ate, as their energy was still merged with his. It added to the enjoyment of the feast. His eyes held Merope's across the table. Food was only one expression of the bliss. Their eyes promised more, each to the other, as the juices of fresh fruits flowed to the center of their bodies like light to the center of the earth.

***

I am back in my bed. I am awake in the early morning darkness and I am ravenous. I find my slippers in the dark and head downstairs to the kitchen. I think only of my hunger and what I will eat. I quickly make a cheese sandwich with a tall glass of soy milk. I need protein. It tastes so scrumptious. Almost as good as the fruit that Sisyphus had been eating. Wait! My journey comes back to me in full detail. I sit down at the kitchen table as I process the fullness of the journey. The food tastes lifeless now compared to my experiences with Merope and Sisyphus.

"Keep eating, Little One. It will help ground you."

I am startled by her voice because I was so engrossed in my experience.

"You need grounding as well. Is there any ice cream in the box that keeps things cold?"

I laugh out loud. Ice cream before breakfast is sort of a taboo for me. I realize what she is doing and I am grateful. How about a nice cup of tea? I feel her acknowledgement and start the water heating. Maybe I'll have one of those bananas while I wait for the water. She starts talking again while I peel the banana.

48

"The work of Merope and Sisyphus was totally misinterpreted by the world. Those few who worked directly with them knew how important the work was. Unfortunately, some did die from the intensity of the energy work. It gave Sisyphus a bad reputation when guests did not survive. He bore it well and even turned it to his advantage. Melicertes and his mother, Ino, were activated to a whole new level of spiritual functioning from the work they did with Merope. The legends say they leaped from a cliff and died and then were resurrected as gods. Their leap was a spiritual leap and their death was a total transformation of their energy. They worked in the Avataric Function after their transformation and that would seem godlike to humanity. Sisyphus started the Isthmian Games to honor the best of Melicertes and his contribution to the work, but also to foster his attributes in humanity."

I've eaten a banana and an orange while she explained the implications of my journey. The tea water is hot. I think I'll have a decaf green tea this morning. Something that's good for my system but not too stimulating. I'm already too stimulated and now I feel full. I take my tea out to the back room to watch the early morning sunlight creep into the world. The deer are feeding in the backyard. I stay quiet so I will not scare them. Avataric Function?

"We will talk of this later, after you have processed the energy from last night. For now, enjoy the memory of your experience, but as always, stay grounded."

Chapter Four

"Little is written about the Seven Sisters, themselves, but their children went out into the world and created patterns of energy that last, even to this day."

The Hooded One

It's been several days since my dream with Merope and Sisyphus. Walking has become a different experience for me. I can feel a direct connection with the Earth after my experience with them. I wait for a hole to open up before me, as if the work continues long after they are gone. I am sitting opposite of The Hooded One and her energy feels all businesslike, which contrasts sharply with the crackling of the fire and the gentle ginger tea before me.

"Businesslike? I am ready to send you on another journey. If that feels like business to you, perhaps we need to have a talk."

I didn't mean to offend. It just feels like you are ready to forego the chitchat tonight.

"Chitchat? Is that what you call our sessions?"

Perhaps you should just send me off to the light before I say anything else to offend you.

She is smiling as she raises her arm.

"At last, you get something right."

And off I go into the light.

***

Maia sat and watched the sun rise over the horizon. Maia was the earth turning…ever turning to bask each region in the sun's light. Maia held earth and sun in her heart as she rose up over the horizon of the Earth Plane. A light like no other. The many expressions of that light flowed out into the Earth Plane irrespective of time and space. She always held the multi-dimensional aspects of herself in her awareness. A breath of awareness became a lifetime. Lifetimes became a moment. All was held within the All in the morning light.

Her beauty and light truly overwhelmed those who traveled paths of Light as flesh. That was part of the reason she preferred the quiet of her cave on this mountain. Mount Kyllini was not only her home, it anchored the nexus of energy created by the Seven Sisters in their work. She anchored their energy through all the dimensions. She held them all in her awareness: Alcyone, who worked with air, even as she lived deep in the ocean; Celaeno, the quiet one, whose meditations guided more than anyone could guess; Electra, hidden on the coast of Ilia after her debacle on Mount Olympus, taught the mysteries of Demeter; Taygeta lived on her mountain; Merope and Sisyphus worked their magic deep into the earth; Sterope's family drew people to the ancient teachings. Their expressions in form were not bound by time and space. Each major human society was held in the energy of the Seven Sisters in one form or another.

Maia breathed in the light and anchored all of the dimensional expressions of her sisters. Her awareness narrowed as her feet carried her back into the cave, away from the light of the world. Her work was anchored deep within the earth. There were times she did not see the sun for days. The focus felt good this morning and she stayed aware of her current form in her current time. It was getting close to the time to embody her work on the Earth Plane. Humans called it bearing a child, but it was ever so much more for Maia. Genetic lines converged down through the ages from her child that would come from a union with Zeus. She paused for a moment as she thought of Zeus. His power was needed for her work, but she hesitated to use it because of how he expressed himself in the world. The subtle energies that she needed to weave her genetic pattern were hard to see in Zeus. Perhaps she should choose another. She really didn't have much more time to ponder on it. Her time was coming.

***

Zeus stood outside Maia's cave for a very long time. Well, it felt long. It felt unbearable. Maia needed his power. Why didn't she call him? She was so beautiful. Now she was one that Hera should worry about. Zeus erased that thought as soon as it crossed

51

his mind. If Hera even got a sniff of it, his life would be unbearable. His life was unbearable without Maia calling him to her. He should just go tell her. No, he didn't dare approach her without her permission. Even with all of his power, Maia's quiet wielding of Source energy gave him pause. He needed to wait to be invited. He didn't like waiting. He had waited eons already. Zeus looked at the entrance to Maia's Cave. It was blurry with all the energy that emanated from within. That energy would make such a nice addition to his collection. He had waited long enough. He was going in.

***

I am sitting with The Hooded One. There is a cup of tea set before me. I obey her silent command to have a sip before I even have a thought. The tea is strong with lots of cream and sugar, my current favorite version of tea. I still hold Zeus and Maia's energy. The tea helps me focus on being with The Hooded One just like it was meant to, I am sure. There is a deep chuckle from The Hooded One. A chuckle?

"I am becoming familiar with your habits, Little One. I am glad that that which grounds you in the world grounds you here where thoughts and time flow differently. I need your focus for a while before we continue on with the union of Zeus and Maia, although I am surprised that a spot of tea could pull you away from witnessing one of the pivotal moments in avataric history."

There's that word again, avataric. What does that mean? It's almost like I can see her eyes close underneath the hood as she inhales and takes her focus to who knows where.

"That place you call The Mysteries, Little One. That place that is pure love as it is expressed in Form."

Her quiet spreads around us. I realize I have stopped breathing. My inhale sounds like a gale in the quiet room that borders the illusion of time and space. I am no longer sure sometimes which is real: my life in the world or here with this being who has touched me so deeply that I feel our connection running through me like the waters running through the earth. I sigh and her awareness returns to me.

"The avatars you know in this world, such as Jesus, Buddha, Mohammad, Krishna, were not the only expressions of Source as Form.

Enlightened beings have held the light as it transforms Earth down through the ages. It matters not if they are called the gods of Mithra, Egypt, Greece, or Rome. These Beings set up energy patterns on the Earth Plane that distilled the magnitude and frequency of Source energy so it could be used, emulated, absorbed and incorporated into the human psyche.

"Be in the stillness with me and feel the mystery of the Entity's intent being made manifest into thought. The Avataric Function worked with the Entity's intent to make it word and deed. Word and deed then fed itself back into intent, creating a cycle that has gone on for longer than the human mind can measure, as Source comes to know itself in the illusion of Form and Separation."

The Hooded One pauses and I reach for my tea. Miraculously, it refills itself here. I try not to gulp down the tea as my brain disengages. Too big... too vast. Thinking of the Entity connection always engulfs me.

"If you think this will engulf you, wait until Zeus and Maia join to create Hermes."

Even as she starts to speak, her voice sounds distant to me as I journey back into the light.

***

Maia felt Zeus enter the cave. She sighed in her human form. It was time. She began to set her intent for the union of their energy. This child had much work to do so it needed the best of their energy. She began to focus her energy with her breathing. She followed her breath into the center of her being. Here, time was eternal and fluid and the patterns flowed from her and through her. She focused on the one about to be created. Their son would be transcendent, beyond the bounds of human thought, his spirit would be made manifest in transition as spirit passed from one condition to another. Maia held the nexus of dimensions so her son could convey and cross dimensions. He would excel and surpass. She breathed out and in as she initiated the sacred energies within her cave and created sacred space. He would be the bearer from one dimension to another. He would step over and beyond limits and boundaries. His energy would transgress... She almost caught her breath on that last one. Here was an anomaly that somehow came from Zeus. Strange that it should be hidden from her sight. Maia

53

breathed in and out and raised her right arm up with her palm facing forward. She was ready for the entrance of Zeus.

***

Zeus walked through the cave slowly. The quality of the rock here was fascinating. Each step revealed a different color and quality that totally held his attention. If it hadn't been for the draw of Maia's energy, he would have stopped and gotten lost in the beauty of the rock. He shook his head and stamped his foot. Focus. He could feel Maia's intent wrap around him as he approached the inner sanctum. He inhaled and exhaled to her rhythm even before he was in her presence. His inhale took him to the core of his energy. He, too, would be creating energy patterns on this day. His son would hold his power to command, but not be bound by it as he was. His son would wield the fire that flowed in Zeus's veins, but it would be controlled through the intellect as creation magic made manifest. Zeus smiled as he bequeathed his masculine magnetism, a gift from father to son, which would surely be appreciated after his son matured.

The focus on his breathing and his energy had occupied Zeus such that he didn't even realize he had entered the inner sanctum until he beheld Maia facing him with her palm raised. She was beautiful beyond words. She was the essence of the feminine made manifest in form. She was … He glanced aside for a brief instance and became enraptured by the stone all around him. What he could create with this! Why, this particular piece was crying out to be molded by his touch. Just a light shave here and a touch of light there and it would truly express its rock nature as light in the world.

Maia was stunned when Zeus stopped his approach to her and became enamored of the rock before him. She knew that Zeus could be predictably unpredictable with creative energy, but this was not anywhere in the patterns. Had Zeus been touched by the madness that infects the gods when their form could not hold their energy? She nearly stopped breathing. She was so incredulous that he would lose his focus at this moment that all she could do was watch as he used the power of his lightning as a fine tuned light and shaved off bits of rock here and there. It was. . . . It was beautiful. Maia breathed in Zeus's energy as he worked his art. This was the energy that she wanted from Zeus for their son. Who would have thought that the thundering Zeus would hold such a delicate touch of creativity? She stepped closer to him and breathed in his essence, which mingled with the physical smell of his musky masculinity. She exhaled and her essence flowed through Zeus and the rock he was carving. She saw the energy taking shape beneath his hands. She reached out and touched Zeus.

Zeus had been so entranced by the rock that he was nearly startled out of his creative trance when he felt her touch. Then their energies blended and one creative energy became another. He was rock being molded by Maia's touch. Quickly, before he got lost in the ecstasy of union, he tucked away a bit of Maia's energy to use later in his creation. Just a bit of her feminine essence stolen, while not exactly stolen, but borrowed. Not exactly borrowed. He needed this for his creativity just as much as he needed ambrosia or air. Focus. He nearly stamped his foot again. Then he became lost in Maia's touch.

Maia felt that tiny something disappear. What was that? Never mind, her energy supply was infinite, just as it seemed Zeus's was as well. He was so creative. She inhaled and then there was only light. Light touching light.

***

It's been a couple of weeks since my journey to witness the union of Zeus and Maia. I have floated through them as if in a dream. I hardly remember the details. I am pretty sure I have been showing up at work but I don't recall what I've done. I do remember becoming fascinated with rocks here and there. They are so spellbinding. I am surprised when fire doesn't jump from my fingertips to carve the rock. I walk through my house and see a cave. I ponder interdimensional reality and again I am surprised when I cannot just pass from one dimension to another.

Have I slept? Have I eaten? I know I have bathed because the touch of the water was divine and I could follow the path of each droplet of water. I have no concept of time. Yet I know that, on some level, my body is going through the small rituals of life. I must have slept. I must have eaten. I feel no hunger. I brush my teeth and get lost in the foamy sensations my toothbrush creates. . . Everything is creation energy. Why didn't I ever see that before? I

55

follow that thought as it creates time and space around me. I am. I am. I am. It is such a magnificent gift to be made manifest.

I feel her calling me, The Hooded One, but her voice in my head becomes a breeze on my face or the touch of fabric on my skin and I lose my way as sound merges with touch merges with thought. "I am coming," I think to her, but another day goes by in that thought.

I place my foot upon the steps to go downstairs. Surely she waits for me in the living room. The interdimensional boundaries feel spongy around me. I am surprised when the hand that steadies me doesn't sink through the wall. If I walked through it, would I be in the room that holds The Hooded One? I come to, facing the wall with my nose pressed against the wall as faint paint smells overwhelm me. I continue down the steps. Surely she is here somewhere. I hear her calling. I search the downstairs. It's only my home. It's a cave. It's a rock to be carved. I sit in the light, only light, and hear her calling.

***

"Little One, you must get grounded."

At last, I sit before her. How did I get here? Am I sleeping or did I truly cross through the dimensional illusion that separates us?

"Focus, Little One. Focus on me. Breathe. Wiggle your toes. Sip your tea. Stay with me this time. We must get you grounded."

I am grounded. I am fine. My toes are fine. My tea is fine. Why is she so worried about me?

"Ignomatius, you are energy drunk and you don't even know it. I had anticipated something like this but I didn't know it would last so long. You have always rebounded so well."

I am rebounding. I bound here. I bound there. I giggle. Suddenly her fingers touch my lips before I can ramble on into oblivion.

"Hush, Little One. I need you to get grounded. Our work is not over."

Her fingertips move from my lips to the crown of my head to my heart. She is chanting in some language I do not know. As soon as I think I do not understand her words, they become clear to me.

"I call to your soul as it speaks through your lips and connects to Source through your head and grounds itself in your form through your heart. I call to the energy that flows through you to release through your lips, through your crown, and through your heart. I call upon your soul to be grounded in form once more in this time and space."

Again, she touches me and I feel that wonderful rock/Zeus/Maia energy flow out into the light it came from and that which is "me", as I know it, well up from my heart and fill me up from top to bottom. I can almost see her face in the hooded robe. She is so close and so intent and suddenly, I feel exhausted.

"Sleep, Little One and dream your own dreams. I will watch over you."

I feel so tired now, but at last I am home in my own skin. What a journey! Thank you, dear Hooded One. Thank you. I sleep and dream my own dreams.

***

I am sitting across from The Hooded One next to the fireplace in her room. As I look around, I notice a picture of Hermes as a baby handing Apollo a lyre. I shudder and turn away.

"If you want to know what the real purpose of the Seven Sisters was on this plane then look to the lives of their children. "

The Hooded One's words rivet my attention.

"Little is written about the Seven Sisters, themselves, but their children went out into the world and created patterns of energy that last, even to this day.

"Hermes was an exceptional god even to the gods. His accomplishments and adventures are legendary. He had his father's charm with the ladies and was nearly as prolific as Zeus in offspring.

"Zeus with his 'stealing' of Maia's energy set up a pattern that has plagued humanity since. Hermes exemplified that pattern even from the cradle as he "stole" cattle from Apollo. Hermes is the patron saint of thieves but the pattern runs much deeper as it is woven through the Darkness of the ages. It is the power to take rather than the power to manifest. "Take" is the operative word here. Instead of trusting that the universe will provide, masculine energy moved into taking what it needed and then wanted. Look at your world now and see that gift of Zeus as it has passed down through the ages."

I am stunned by the power of the words from The Hooded One. I thought the gods knew everything. Wouldn't they have seen the consequences of their actions and created change if it was needed?

"They did create change. It was the nature of their being to create change. They could see the energy patterns as they would evolve but there was a factor that no one could predict. That factor was the free will of humanity. Humans made choices that affected the energy patterns just as deeply."

Like what?

"Look at the choices humans have made around pain. Pain is just a side effect of learning, but humanity has so focused on it that it has become a major thread in your consciousness."

The no pain, no gain concept.

"More than that! They have glorified suffering. Look at the image of Jesus on the cross as the symbol of Christianity. Why that symbol?"

Well, he died for our sins.

"And wouldn't a symbol of Jesus ascending into heaven with joy on his face be just as apt? People focus on the pain to the exclusion of joy. It was never meant to be that way. The message of Jesus was about love and tolerance and forgiveness. How different would the world be today if those who worship the Christ had focused on the love of God rather than the fear of God?

"Humanity is a golden thread woven into the energy of the gods. Humanity was a gift to the gods. A gift that has changed the very fabric of the Earth Plane as it is manifested through the Divine Feminine and the Divine Masculine. That fabric is love and it is woven by the hands of love. When humanity lives that love within that fabric they are being god-like as they can access and understand Divine Energy. Love is and always has been the key."

The Hooded One is glowing as she talks. I can feel waves of energy emanating from her. A phrase goes through my head. "I can feel the love." It takes on a whole new meaning. There is so much joy, so much love, I can no longer hold my focus here.

***

I awaken. I drift a little bit and start to remember my dreams. I could see Love marching across the planet making change. Love would turn into little keys that people would pick up and then the people would feel empathy and compassion for all the creatures of the planet; it was so beautiful. I thought about the world I saw on the news and then the world in my dreams and wondered where the keys are now?

"They are there waiting, Little One. Humanity just needs to pick them up. They need to choose love. That has been the message of all the Masters sent to this planet."

I feel The Hooded One's presence in my mind. She is a comfort and a joy to me. How our relationship has changed over the months.

"How you have changed, Little One."

It is true. I have changed and it is for the better, but I still like my cup of tea and it is time to get up. Maybe I will find one of those keys today.

"You are a key, Ignomatius. You are a key. Our journeys will lead you to unlocking that which is within you that is part of the stars. Enjoy your morning, but know that we will move beyond all understanding you have of the world and what is beyond."

Chapter Five

"Humanity has embraced the illusion. Those who recognize and honor the balance and dance of the Divine Masculine and Divine Feminine are in a minority, ridiculed and reviled." The Hooded One

Once again, I am sitting with The Hooded One in her study. There is no need to follow her here now as my awareness shifts while I sleep. I ponder that change as she gently scans my energy. Who knows what she finds there?

"I am looking to see that you are ready for the next journey, Little One. I think you might be ready for another dimensional leap."

I laugh and reply that I think I might have made one too many dimensional leaps already. She smiles at my thought, but her answer is serious.

"Ignomatius, you have only just begun to explore the dimensions. The Seven Sisters were interdimensional beings on your plane. They were manifested in some form in nearly every major culture of what you think of as ancient history. The Greek story that we have been exploring is one of those versions. There were manifested versions of the Seven Sisters in the current regions of Australia, Egypt, India, Peru, Japan, Hawaii, Norway and more. Even though they were manifested with different names, it was the same energy of beings who appeared throughout time and space. Human consciousness and even the earth plane were changed as a result of their presence."

I can feel the power emanating from The Hooded One as she speaks. It rolls over me but my mind cannot fathom the scope that her words and her energy are trying to convey. How could they be everywhere at once? How could they be many individuals in form and still be the Seven Sisters? The Hooded One leans toward me.

"Ignomatius, in your own life, you are the many and the one at the same time. Look at your life. You are the worker, mentor, relative, friend,

business associate, adventurer, and spiritual seeker. Each role requires different aspects of yourself to come into play, yet you are still you. The energy of what you call the gods is just the same, except that it can be made manifest in several versions in different times and places and still be the same energy. The limitations of Form shift and change as higher vibrational beings work within the Earth Plane."

Again, her intensity rolls over me. I can see the Pleiades constellation entering the earth plane and the stars breaking up into smaller versions of the same energy, landing in different times and places upon the Earth. It sort of feels like they become mother, sister, daughter, aunt, and cousin all at the same time; and yet, they are as whole and complete as when they manifested their energy in Form. I step back from the vision and see The Hooded One in front of me. I can feel her satisfaction with my understanding.

"Ignomatius, this may feel big but it is still only a small step into the greater understanding of Light and Love as it is made manifest on this plane.

"The pattern that Zeus created by taking some of the goddesses' energy to fulfill something that was wanting within himself was found in stories from other cultures as well. It is time to explore alternative versions of the sisters. Tonight you are off to the prehistoric age in Australia, whose ancient name has been lost in the annals of time."

She raises her arm and I am off to another adventure.

***

I found myself in the middle of the desert in the darkness of night. I could almost feel the deep chill of the desert wind. The stars above me were imbedded in a velvety indigo rug. It feels like I could reach up and touch the sky. The beauty of the Australian Outback night took my breath away.

In the distance I saw a light, so I walked closer to get a view. It was a small camp fire and a figure huddled close to the meager warmth. As I got closer, I could hear muttering in a deep timbre. Must be a man. As I listened the words became clearer. "I hear you. You are mine. Come closer, I hear you. You are mine. Come closer." I stopped. Not sure if the man knew I was there and was talking to me or something else. As I stood there, I could hear a tinkling in the distance. Not quite bells. More like the sound of wind chimes and the sound approached us.

I looked back at the man in the fire light and could make out small details. He was short of stature, but powerfully built and there was a surge of power radiating from him that had nothing to do with the fire. His clothes were ragged. A large sharpened stick was by his side. He projected the deep whisper into the night and I could feel the raw magic mingled into the flow of words. "I hear you. You are mine. Come closer."

I did not feel drawn by the power in the words, but someone did. I could hear them approaching as the chimes grew louder. Then they were upon us. A force of light and magic traveling through the desert night. The seven sisters, pale and cold like the distant stars. Their long hair frozen into icicles that gently chimed with their movement across the land.

As they explored the terrain, they made artless gasps of delight as they came upon small, bright rocks or thorny clusters of bushes or twisted succulent witchity grubs. Each sister sharing with the others her find. Their pale beauty weaving through the night as they moved with the love of sisters on adventure together. "See what I have found. Look at this. Taste this sister."

They came upon the man sitting at the fire and gathered around him in wonder. I could see the frost of his breath as he was surrounded by their pale light, his dark leathery skin made soft in their radiance. His eyes glowed with need and desire. I felt a pang of warning as I saw his eyes, but it was too late to warn the sisters as I saw him extend forth small sticks with roasted lizard to them as an act of homage. The sisters inhaled the fragrance of the fire, the man, the lizard on the stick and their light sparkled. The man's litany became louder and darker and I could see his energy wrapped around the sticks in dark bands of grasping hands.

Two sisters reached forward and took the offering. As they bit into the lizard they became transfixed. The rest of the sisters marveled and danced around in the fire light and then continued on into the night, not seeing the ones left behind, as they were held in thrall by the sorcerer's magic.

***

I am back with the Hooded One, chilled more from the act of betrayal than the cold of the Australian night or the frosty appearance of the sisters who were not of this earth.

The Hooded One sits quietly as I gather myself from my journey. Finally she speaks, interrupting the quiet of our room and I realize from her voice that she is disquieted.

"Wurrunnah was a great hunter but much like your nerds of today, he did not have good people skills."

I am startled by her use of the word nerds. It must show on my face because she pauses.

"Nerds is one of those wonderful slang words that project a perfect image of a stereotype – skilled yet shy. Mastery in a technology but lacking in social graces. Perhaps willing to bend the rules to get what they want as Wurrunnah.

"Wurrunnah wanted a woman to take care of him but he wanted more than that, he wanted the power of the sisters. He lusted for their beauty and grace. He knew their ethereal minds held him in little consequence. It burned in his heart to be spurned when he should be honored for his great hunting expertise. So he set out to capture and enthrall what he could not attract.

"According to the Australian legend, the sisters came to Earth from the stars via a giant pine tree that grew into the heavens. This tree is known in esoteric circles as the Tree of Life, the pathway into and out of the Earth plane. The Tree embodies the elements of some of the greatest secrets of spiritual knowing.

"In the Australian version of the sisters' legend, Wurrunnah wanted wives to take care of him, but he really wanted their knowledge of the Tree and the access it would give him to greater power."

So he was a lot like Orion from the Greek legend: the greatest hunter after the best game.

"Exactly."

The Hooded One paused and let the silence stretch in our conversation. I sat and contemplated the scene in the desert. The sense of wrongness still lingered as I saw the two sisters frozen by the campfire as the rest of them went on their way through the night. Another version of a man taking the power he wanted, instead of following the inner path that winds its way to our spiritual wholeness.

The Hooded One interrupts my thoughts. *"The duality of masculine and feminine was not meant to be the power of one over the other. Literally, the one cannot be without the other. Mastery of that duality is a merging of that which is masculine and feminine back into Oneness. Masculine energy on the Earth plane has forgotten or ignored its role in the creator process. Feminine energy has relinquished its power just like the two sisters who ate the poisoned lizard and couldn't move. Their power still remained, but it lay forgotten and unused."*

Well, not everyone forgets or misuses the power.

"True, but the social mores and cultural practices around the world support the masculine power over the feminine. Humanity has embraced the illusion. Those who recognize and honor the balance and dance of the Divine Masculine and Divine Feminine are in a minority, ridiculed and reviled."

Is that why the sisters no longer come to visit the Earth? People trying to steal their power?

"Where did that question come from?"

Well, it seemed like the sisters were everywhere and then left, never to return. Their power and beauty were hungered after in almost all the stories. They were even chased into the heavens once they left.

"Humanity needed time to mature. The gifts of the gods and goddesses were abused by too many. They are still being abused. It is time for another shift and the interdimensional beings will return to work with human beings once again."

Interdimensional beings?

"A more accurate description of the gods and goddesses. Source itself is a multi-dimensional matrix of energy that encompasses the known and unknown manifestations of Itself."

That's a lot to think about.

"Well, sleep on it and we'll see where this journey takes us."

As I fade away into my dreams, I think I am sleeping already. I hear the Hooded One's voice respond *"All illusion, Ignomatius, all illusion."*

***

As I am running my errands the next day, I am at the supermarket and witness a scene where a husband is berating his wife for not doing something right. She appears to be crestfallen and mumbles a reply back to him. As the exchange happens, I can hear the crackling of Wurrunnah's fire and see the dark energy surrounding the woman in the market. I also see how the dark energy has the man tangled up. Is he directing the energy or is it directing him? As I watch them play out an age-old scenario, I realize that we are all ensnared by our beliefs of what is masculine and what is feminine. Our archetypes of appropriate behavior for both male and female roles binds us all to the illusion of separation.

All around me I can see the dark hands of sorcery reaching out to take more energy, but the hands are bound by a craving that need not be there if we all recognized and accepted our inner divinity and connection.

It's been several days since I've seen The Hooded One. Life has been hectic with deadlines at work and holidays with the family. At least we are through the holidays, with my family fussing about my being single and "where oh where" are the grandchildren. How could I possibly find someone who understands my connection with The Hooded One? Some of my friends know, but to them it is a weird thing that I am into. At least they don't suggest that I check into a psych ward like my parents did when I tried to talk to them about it. Not a topic of conversation at home anymore. My connection with The Hooded One may seem like an aberration to my family, but it is a safe haven for me. And the tea is good as well. I hear a faint chuckle in my head that comes from a comfy room deep within my psyche.

I remember her last words to me: "All is illusion." I think about all the sages and enlightened beings I have read about. They all had a message of love and compassion. Is it so different that my teacher exists only in my head? Her message of love and her deep understanding of the human psyche are a gift to me that I will always treasure.

***

At last I am back with The Hooded One with a cup of ginger tea before me. The pungent smell of the ginger wafts around me and stimulates my awareness. The energy of The Hooded One permeates the room. Quiet power balanced with compassion and love. I wonder once again who is this being that has become my friend and teacher?

"Leave a woman her secrets, Ignomatius. Truly there is no way to explain who and what I am until you leave your form on the Earth plane. Then we will have a cup of tea in our light bodies. For now, let's focus on Wurrunnah. His bold attempt to capture the sisters did not go quite as planned, as you will see."

She lifts her arm and points to the light. I am wearing a sweater tonight. I thank my subconscious mind for thoughtful comforts as I am whisked off to the Australian Outback once more.

***

I arrive once more at the scene of the campfire, only this time there are three figures huddled around its warmth. I sense that we are many leagues away from the site of the capture. Wurrunnah doesn't want the two sisters found by their powerful siblings.

I watch him and see his dark energy flowing around the sisters. They are chatting about everyday things but his energy has the slimy feel of a man reaching for that which is beyond his measure to have. He inches closer to the sister sitting next to him. Her pale radiance does not outshine the firelight as it once did, although her beauty remains eternal. He reaches to touch her arm and pull her close. As his hand touches her, his face twists into a grimace. He jumps back and shakes his hand, now nearly frozen from the touch of the heavenly sister. He stalks around the fire holding his hand and cursing the sisters for being useless. He just wants to be nice to them and they hurt him. The sisters make sounds of comfort but do not attempt to console him. There will be no consummation to quench his physical desires tonight, and not possibly ever.

As I listen to Wurrunnah mumble, I can hear him planning a stronger spell of sorcery to allow him to have his way with the sisters. It will require some special ingredients. They will start gathering them in the morning light.

***

Wurrunnah has returned from hunting with a couple of wombats and a koala. He places them on a rock near the campsite and gestures to the sisters to prepare them for eating. Then he goes to inspect the ingredients that they have gathered for the spell. He holds each herb to feel its strength and purity. He will need only the best to overcome the strength of the sisters' connection to the stars. Then they will be his forever. The herbs speak to him of their power and he wraps his energy around them to prepare them for the potion. As he goes through the pile, he realizes he needs to add something else. Something so powerful and rare that it will enhance the effect of the potion beyond the sisters' ability to combat.

He stares at the sisters as they prepare the food. They are kind and gentle with each other but detached from their task at the same time. Their willowy forms fill his heart with lustful intentions. Their long hair still freezes in long icicles that tingle and fill the void of silence in the world around them. The tingling sounds make him angry and his eyes glow with the depth of his lust mixed with anger. As he stares at the sisters he is inspired for the one ingredient he needs to complete the potion.

Everyone knows that the sisters descend to Earth each time they visit via a great pine tree that touches the heavens. When they return to the stars the tree catches them up and carries them back to the stars. He needs some bark from that tree, but it only appears for the sisters and the ascending masters.

"Leave dinner!" Go and get me some pine bark now!" His rough voice startles the sisters and they drop the knives they were using to prepare the animals.

They reply with their lilting voices, speaking as one: "But we must not go to the pine forest. We might not come back."

Wurrunnah literally snarls in frustration, like the big cats he hunts. "I said go, you will return to me with plenty of pine bark from the tree you use to come from the heavens." The sisters trembled at the anger in his voice. "But we are not sure we can find it without all of our sisters around us."

Wurrunnah picked up two combos and flung them at the feet of the sisters. They jumped aside to miss being impaled by their sharp edges. "Do not return until you have the pine bark, I need a lot." Wurrunnah glared at them until they picked up the combos and ran away. He would have his way with both of them. They would like it. His black heart followed them as they ran toward the forest. The bonds of sorcery remained quite strong enough to hold them to his will.

***

I am back with The Hooded One. Wurrunnah's dark anger is fresh in my mind. I shudder at the image.

"Humanity has lived with the shadow aspects of the Divine Masculine for so long that they consider it normal. The unbalanced greed and lust in your world today has eaten away at the health and welfare of civilization to the point where whole countries stand ready to fail. This pattern of the male taking what he wants, while the female acquiesces to his wishes, has become a liability to humanity.

"It is time for humanity to wake up and remember the wholeness of their spiritual nature. The negative versions of gender roles must be recreated in balance based on love and sharing."

How do we do that when the shift in power is so far the other way? What can I do that will make a difference to some billionaire intent on squeezing every last dime from me so they can buy art for their tenth mansion? The bitterness in my voice surprises even me. The Hooded One sits back.

"Take a deep breath, Little One. You already hold the power. It is in your heart to choose love over fear, to honor your spiritual being, to honor the earth. As each one of humanity recognizes the power of love, change will happen. Extending compassion and kindness to those around you will allow the change to happen more quickly.

"Wurrunnah held the two sisters in his dark sorcery, but when they went to the forest and cut into the first pine, the Tree of Life recognized them, and carried them up into the heavens, back to their sisters. Spirit awaits you to lift you up. It resides in all the life force around you and within you. It is a choice to recognize and honor Spirit over the mundane. That recognition can come from the smallest act or the greatest pain. Choose to not live in the illusion of limitation. The wealthiest billionaires are bound to the illusion just as much as the homeless man on the street. Those who have so much and take from those who have so little are acting from fear and limitation.

"When you choose love, no one has power over you. When you choose balance and compassion, you change the world. When you are living as Spirit in Form, possessions do not possess you. When you move beyond the stereotypes of masculine and feminine, you stand in the light as co-creator of your universe. That universe can be the smallest hut in a homeless village or a grand villa on the Mediterranean. When you are standing in wholeness, the illusion of fear and lack does not rule you. This is the change already happening in the world around you. The ones in power who rule with dark hearts know that change is coming and they cling to the old patterns. Manipulation through fear is their greatest weapon, not the bombs or their control of the financial markets. Fear rules them, but love awaits. Now is the time for humanity to recognize their true nature as spiritual beings. It is a

revolution that is happening and it is only a choice away for each and every one of you."

I am stunned by the passion and fervor of The Hooded One's homily. The room filled with light as she progressed in her answer. My heart leaps in my chest with hope.

"There is more than hope, Little One. All the powers of the universe are focusing on your planet to help shepherd humanity's next step in evolution. The veil of illusion is falling from the human psyche and the awareness and connection to Source will be readily available to all who simply ask."

Wow! I am speechless.

"You can wander the desert with the dark-hearted Wurrunnah, or ascend to the heavens with the sisters. The choice is yours."

Well for right now, I think I will finish my cup of tea, if you don't mind.

"Wander the world with a cup of tea made with love, Ignomatius. It's a grand adventure, this world of yours. Full of beauty and horror, vast resources and deadly climates. This world is a gift to humanity. Use it wisely so that humanity is a gift to the world."

We sit quietly after that and sip our tea. At some point, I drift off and wake up in the universe of my bedroom full of hope and love.

Chapter Six

The human spirit's ability to overcome adversity is a gift to the gods and of the gods."
               The Hooded One

"How much do you know about the Hindu gods and goddesses?"

The Hooded One's abrupt question catches me off guard. I have barely tasted my tea.

How much do I know about Hinduism? As her question echoes through my mind, I see a version of the Pleiades break off and land on the continent of India. The seven stars merge briefly with the seven Rishis and then the Pleiades emerge as six, not seven stars. I am mystified as I sit and watch the dance of the stars. How does this relate to the Hindu gods and goddesses?

As I watch, a smaller version of The Hooded One appears in my vision among the dancing stars and walks toward me. I realize I am no longer aware of the chair or the room. I am standing next to The Hooded One in a field of stars. It helps to have her next to me as a reference of up and down. I breathe a sigh of relief and then stop. There is no air in space, but I just experienced breathing. I reach out to touch the darkness around us as if it has a tangible presence. I am touching it, yet not touching it. I feel a warning coming from The Hooded One.

"Don't try to touch the stars, Ignomatius. You aren't ready for that yet."

Where are we? What happened to our room? How can we be here? I feel the gaze of The Hooded One upon me. The stars swirl around her. Is she a star? Have I finally died to come to this place? Again, I feel that touch of The Hooded One's presence and then she speaks.

"Our room where we meet in the subterranean chamber of your consciousness is a construct, a way for your mind to translate our

communication so that it understands and feels comfortable. It is no more or less real than the place we stand now. As light explores itself in different vibrational forms, it appears in constructs that make sense to the mind that is perceiving it. You'll come to understand that what you call earth, or home, or reality is where you find yourself at this moment. It is all light. It is all love.

"For you to understand the true meaning of the Hindu mythology, I needed you to stand here among the stars to be able to hold the greater perspective, as your mind explores the higher dimensional aspects of the Seven Sisters."

Now I'm getting dizzy as I watch the stars twirl and swirl. I feel The Hooded One touch my hand and then we're back in our room with the fire crackling in the fireplace. I can see the sparks dancing in the same patterns as the stars. I look away. I feel the gentle touch of The Hooded One in my mind and turn back to look at her comforting form. She is giving me instructions.

"For the next journey, you need to prepare your form so that it is functioning at its highest level. Let's try a week of a cleansing fast with daily meditation and walking. For the fast, you will drink only clear liquids from 9:00 PM until noon the next day. No caffeine or sugar. If you drink juices, cut them in half with water. From noon to nine at night, we need you to eat only rice and vegetables. No animal products, and that includes milk, cheese, and eggs. No heavy spices. Small amounts of salt, pepper, and lemon are acceptable."

I think of my refrigerator. I'm going to have to make a trip to the store tomorrow.

"Start at nine tomorrow night and follow this diet for a week. Walk at least ½ hour outside every day, preferably in silence. Will you do this for me?"

Well, I guess it is herbal teas for me this week and no trips to Starbucks.

"Ah-h, but we can still watch Star Trek or have you graduated to Battlestar Galactica yet?"

We laugh as I drift into my regular dreams, though I would hardly call them regular dreams since there are stars twirling and swirling through all of them.

***

The cleansing fast goes easier than I thought it would. I've done different kinds of fasts before. At least on this one, I get to eat a moderate amount of food. My energy is much lighter after a week on this diet. The hardest part was the caffeine headaches. I do miss my English breakfast tea.

***

I am standing among the stars again with The Hooded One. She is holding my hand; this is surprising since she so rarely touches me.

"It is a way to keep you anchored, Little One. What we are about to witness is another high energy event. Actually, it's a series of high energy events."

Even as she speaks my attention is drawn to an especially bright area of the stars. As I focus there, I can see an image of the Earth, surrounded by seven balls of light. I don't think it is the Seven Sisters, since I would recognize the signature of their energy.

"It is the energy of the Seven Rishis as they were called in Hindu tradition. They are sages of the highest order in the Earth plane. They are considered planetary spirits for the Earth, yet their energy is also connected to Ursa Major, as is the Pleiades."

As I watch, I see the energy of the Pleiades coming to the Earth plane and merging with the energy of the Rishis. I am deeply touched on some level at this merging of masculine and feminine energy. The brightness of the orbs intensifies so much I look away for a few seconds. Then as I turn back, six orbs of light float gently down to the Earth. I look askance at The Hooded One.

"It is the mystery of the missing sister. We will return to this later."

Her voice is a whisper of light. She points to another section of the stars. I feel a huge presence but it's not connected to a specific star. Then my senses focus on Phruva, the Pole Star. A flash of light, like a shooting star, enters into Phruva, and after a brief pause flows out and down to the Earth, landing on the continent of India. At that point, it divides and becomes four rivers of light upon the Earth. My heart feels like it is being washed within that light as I witness the scene before me. I am enthralled and ready to step forth among the stars to follow the rivers' light from the highest of the mountains to the depths of the ocean. A light touch on my arm distracts me.

"Come, Ignomatius. You have witnessed enough here."

72

We are back in our room. A cup of tea awaits me on the table. I take a sip without thinking. Strong ginger tea laced with honey. It helps me focus on the here and now instead of me flowing in rivers across India to the ocean.

"You just witnessed the birth of Ganga upon the Earth. Her energy was held in the light of Shiva before it was released onto the Earth in order to prepare her energy such that it could manifest on the Earth. High vibrational energy cannot always be held in Form if it is not refined and slowed in its vibrational nature. Ganga's energy washes and heals. It flows and transforms."

A deep sigh escapes my lips. I want to be washed and healed by Ganga.

"Perhaps another day, Little One. Today's journey is but a preamble to the true heart of the light you are here to witness. Have another sip of tea. How are you doing so far?"

Just a preamble? The strong ginger overwhelms my senses and distracts me from my yearning to be washed in light. I am grounded again. The Hooded One nods in satisfaction.

"You are progressing nicely, Little One. Light agrees with you."

So does ginger tea. As I look up from blowing on the hot tea to cool it down for my next sip, I see The Hooded One's arm pointing. Wow! We have journeyed beyond anything I had imagined today, and still she is sending me off to the next vision. As I merged into the light I could hear her voice.

"Wow is an understatement."

***

The scene before my eyes is so astounding that I just stare for several minutes before I can even process what I am seeing.

There is a baby on a mound of gold. Not just a baby but a six headed godling surrounded by the Seven Sisters. No, wait, there are only six of them, and they are mothering this child. Each one of the sisters is acting like she is the mother. I can feel the energetic connection of mother to child emanating from all six to the baby. It is so bizarre to me that I close my eyes and shake my head. I open them and look around. We are standing in a bed of reeds near a river, not just any river! I can sense the healing energy of Ganga and realize I am in India! We are in the middle of nowhere in a bed of reeds. Six of the seven sisters are nursing a six headed god child that rests upon a mountain of gold. I start a deep breathing exercise to try to ground my energy.

Suddenly I feel the gaze of all six heads of the godchild upon me; its voice is in my head, so loud my head hurts. I do not understand the words but I get the name, Kartikeya, Son of Shiva. And I get Krittikas. Krittikas are the sisters, no the mothers. The images and words are too much. My head hurts beyond belief. I must leave. NOW!

***

I wake up in my own bed. It is still dark and I have a massive headache. I stumble into the bathroom to get some ibuprofen. As I pour a glass of water from the faucet, I feel Ganga flowing near me. I can't focus with my head hurting so much. Take the pills. Drink the water. Go back to bed. I order myself around and somehow make it back to bed.

I turn on a light hypnosis CD to give myself something to focus on besides the pain. Somehow I fall back to sleep. Mercifully, it is a deep, dreamless sleep.

I wake up grumpy with a memory of the headache pain still fresh. Although it seems to have passed, I hurt all over. Groaning, I get up and gingerly walk down the stairs. Ginger! Ginger tea would be good this morning. My mind shies away from why I want ginger tea. I try not to think as I prepare the tea. The rich, pungent taste of the tea stimulates more than just my taste buds as I remember my experiences from last night. The stars merging. The baby on the pile of gold. The loud voice in my head. Again, I shy away from the words.

"Little One, try not to go there in your thoughts until we are together again."

There is an image of a curtain closing on a stage. Mercifully, the scene in my head is gone! Thank you, dear Hooded One.

"You are welcome, Ignomatius. You did well last night. Don't let the after effects color the depth of your experiences."

Maybe I'll do a few stretches after my tea to get the kinks out.

"Your kinks are embedded in your soul. Stretching is good but your "kinks" won't go away."

We both smile and enjoy the morning light.

***

The Hooded One is waiting for me, sitting in the easy chair with the fire burning brightly. I wonder what she does when we are not here. She turns her head toward me.

"I am light, Little One. Just light. The same way you are."

I complain about an achy back and being light.

"One of the joys of flesh that I do not need to experience. Sit and have a cup of tea. Tea helps everything. So first we are going to focus on Kartikeya and turn down that voice in your head. It's too loud even for me."

I have no doubt that she could hear his voice above all my thoughts. The volume has not decreased with time.

"He wanted so much to communicate with you. Baby gods are still learning their powers. He has planted a seed that will grow later. Visualize a seed and plant it in a corner of your mind. Good. Now water it and then feel the sun shining on it."

It's growing already!

"Assure Kartikeya that you will nurture and grow the gift he has given to you."

I see the godling in my mind and tell him how grateful I am for his gift and that I will let it grow within me. The loud voice in my head recedes. That is so much better.

"Kartikeya was the son of Shiva, not just any godling."

So why were the Seven Sisters nursing him?

"There are several versions to the story but they all agree that the Seven Sisters were the only ones whose energy was high enough to sustain contact with Shiva's seed and son. Imagine, if you will, pure creation energy force coming to the planet without any preparation beforehand. The nature of high vibrational energy tends to melt the physical world around it. The impact of such energy on the physical world is immense."

But we all come from creation force.

"Creation force energy that has taken eons to evolve. The physical realm energy is a very slow vibration. The energy that the concept of Shiva represents is so highly refined that its effect on the physical world seems disastrous to the human eye. The son of God is stepped down energy, sent to this planet for a specific purpose. The story goes that Kartikeya came here to fight a demon who was wreaking havoc. Have you ever fought a demon, Ignomatius?"

No, I don't think I could defeat a demon.

"On the contrary, humanity fights demons all the time. The demon of addiction. The demon of depression. The demon of poverty. They are constantly plagued by such demons. Many times they win, and many times they lose, but they get back up and try again. The human spirit's ability to overcome adversity is a gift to the gods and of the gods."

There is so much wonder and joy emanating from The Hooded One as she speaks. In my mind's eye, I can see the gift of Kartikeya flowing out to the world, the spirit to overcome the worst demons we might ever encounter. I am so grateful for that gift. I have used it many times in this life. The Hooded One is glowing a golden light as I process the meaning of Kartikeya's story. Once again, I see the baby godling laying on a mound of gold. The volume of his voice is much lower now. He seems to be a very content baby as he is nurtured by the Krittikas. So what happened to that pile of gold? The Hooded One shakes her head and the glow disappears.

"You are human after all. The pile of gold disappears from the story and from the Earth plane. There have been manifestations of gods and goddesses that have left their mark upon the planet for all time though."

Really? Like who and what?

"Taygeta, for one."

The Hooded One is raising her arm and pointing towards the light. Off I go again.

Chapter Seven

You are a co-creator of the universe and as such, are as much a god as any which your species names and creates."   The Hooded One

It's an odd experience this time. I'm not really seeing anything. It feels like I am contained in a bubble. There is nothing to see. Yet I am not in darkness and not in the light. I take a deep breath. There is no sense of movement. Where am I? Just as I am about to panic, I hear a voice that is not a voice. How do I explain the non-experience of this place?

"Relax, Ignomatius. You are being held within my consciousness. We are in a state of being."

I recognize this voice. It's one of the sisters. I sift through what I know, but cannot pinpoint which one. How can you be suspended in a state of being anyway? This is worse than standing in a field of stars with no reference to up or down. I take another deep breath. How does one of the sisters know the name The Hooded One uses with me? Again the voice speaks, closer, like she is standing next to me. Yet there is no sense of standing and no one that I can see.

"Ignomatius, we are aware of your presence, especially after your encounter with Electra and the Weaver. Once you come to the attention of the Weaver, your thread of light glows like it has been polished to a fine shine."

I am sorry but I cannot place which sister you are.

"In this plane, we are one. Your presence lends a sense of individuated oneness. Naming you brings me so close to naming myself. How odd that concept of name…or self. Self exists. Self can be expressed. Self…"

The voice is trailing off even as I feel the energy around me bunch and gather, concentrating itself around me. It is so beautiful. I sense structure in a way I have never experienced it before. The not-light around me is a concept that I know well, but not in a way that I can grasp.

"Don't grasp. Be!"

I am. I am a mathematical equation. All around me are the pure thought forms of the equations of the universe. The order. The joy of oneness is held within each progression of finite and infinite equations. As I watch the equations flow by, they begin to coalesce into a point, a point of being made manifest.

"My name is Taygeta."

I am witnessing the birth of Taygeta on the physical plane. It is so different from Maia's birth. Even as I think this thought, the equations around me are changing rapidly.

"Ignomatius, I find that while a point holds the now and contains within itself all of Source, it cannot contain all that is my expression of Source. I am more."

A second point emerges from the dizzying array of equations flowing around me. A line forms from one point to the other; discrete from point to point and yet infinite as now connects to the next moment and becomes more. Is that a hint of breath that I feel? Form breathes from point to point, in and out. There is now direction in the equations around me.

"The experience of movement is exhilarating! Form holds such delights. I can be and be... and be again!"

As I watch, a third point appears upon the plane. The line becomes a triangle. We experience two dimensionality. I say we, for I am definitely a part, even as I am within. The light around me brightens as if I had been in darkness. Once again, I feel an expansion as Taygeta's awareness moves from point to point to point. Equations are flowing into each point and out again to the next, a steady stream of precise brilliance that becomes one and then another. There is a sense of ...

"Duality! That which Is becomes All which becomes Is!"

The cryptic remark makes sense as the equations define two dimensional reality. The pure mathematical oneness of Taygeta coalesces into a point and then expands into the other two points. There is the sense of a gasp as one recognizes the other. Startled by its own awareness of self, a fourth point emerges. Light bursts into three dimensions and a tetrahedron is formed. I feel consciousness becoming personality. Equations become form. Oneness becomes individuated. Time to step back and let the state of being that is Taygeta become the goddess upon the Earth Plane.

I am standing on a mountain overlooking one of the most beautiful valleys I have ever seen: wild, raw beauty. Lush growths of trees that cascade to deep crevasses of verdant darkness holding the very secrets of life. My senses are stunned and overwhelmed. Who knows how long I stand and stare? How does the mind process such beauty and pristine expression of the divine? As I stand, immobilized by the wonder of the earth's beauty, I become aware of a presence next to me. It is more than presence. The three dimensional expression of Taygeta is a large pyramid of stone imbedded into the mountain itself. Again, my mind is thrown into chaos as my physical senses try to construct the expression of that which is unknowable into that which is form. I can feel Taygeta's consciousness anchored within the stone, the mathematical precision of her beingness expressed as three dimensional reality. I am so small in the presence of such a magnificent being, dwarfed by the pyramid held within the wild beauty of mountains covered by lush forests, emanating life force so strong and wild that even the rocks beneath my feet have living presence. I become smaller and smaller as the life force around me takes on the huge surge of Taygeta's emergence into being on the Earth Plane.

There is a breath. The life force around me breathes with it. There is movement. The life force around me moves with it. There is awareness. The life force around me reaches toward that awareness. I marvel at the impact of Taygeta's energy on all that surrounds us.

"Your energy has the same impact as mine, Ignomatius, as does all of humanity. It is all one. All is connected. Each breath and thought go into the cosmic matrix that you saw as mathematical equations. Separation is the illusion, and the time fast approaches for that illusion to fall away from people's consciousness."

Why do you communicate with me directly when none of the others have?

"You need what I offer. Call on me when you need help. I think you will find it most beneficial."

I feel her presence turn away from me. Her awareness goes out to the beauty that surrounds us.

"I have much to contemplate. I will eventually take on human form when I am ready. You may leave now. Our connection will remain."

Abruptly, I find myself back in my bed. Ouch, that hurts. Feeling small takes on a new meaning as I lay in darkness surrounded by simple furniture instead of the wonders of the coastal mountains of ancient Greece. I drift back to sleep in hopes of dreams that will take me there once more.

***

I sit across from The Hooded One in the hominess of our retreat. It comforts me to be here in ways that nothing else in my life gives comfort.

"Even better than mashed potatoes, Little One?"

Even better than tea, I reply, as I sip on the jasmine tea that is in the cup tonight. The transition from pure spiritual being to human being was pretty rough on me this last time. It's been days since I witnessed the birth of Taygeta and I still feel small. Small is not an adequate word. Miniscule? Insignificant?

"When you accept your humanity as the true gift it is, you will no longer have such rough transitions, Ignomatius. You are a co-creator of the universe and as such, are as much a god as any which your species names and creates."

So we create our gods?

"There is a matrix of divine energy that has awareness and conscious intent for the Earth Plane. It is too vast and complex for the human mind to comprehend, so humanity names it and creates beings who express portions of that divine matrix. There is a certain comfort level attained with naming."

Like I call you The Hooded One? What is your name anyway? The Hooded One remains quiet and politely ignores my question. So Taygeta talked directly to me. What does that really mean?

"You have work to do together, just as you and I work together."

And that work is?

"I am sure it will be revealed in time."

I so love being a human guinea pig.

"It seems that you are not ready for more tonight. Your psyche needs rest."

My psyche needs answers. Again, there is a polite waiting as I stare at the blankness of The Hooded One's face. She reaches out and touches my hand. I am so startled that I react badly to her gesture of comfort.

"It's all right, Ignomatius. You struggle against your human limitations instead of experiencing the joy that is the gift available to you."

The gift?

"I am light. You are a hundred different beings every minute. You breathe. You laugh. You love. You grieve. I am light. Your human expression of Source is a gift to Light."

Most days it does not feel like a gift.

"You are so grumpy tonight. Perhaps you should spend a few days out in nature. Ride your bike. Hike. Go kayaking on your favorite river. We will talk again in a few days."

You mean do something that isn't my spiritual work?

"It's all spiritual work, Little One. You were in a state of pure being with Taygeta. Now you are in a state of doing. Go do and love it. The exercise and connection with nature will ease the ache of transition from one state to the other."

***

It's been several days since I have spoken to The Hooded One. I have been very busy working and playing. I feel much more balanced now. Perhaps tonight I will visit The Hooded One in my dreams.

***

She waits so patiently for me in our cozy room. Why did I want to stay away from here? I feel her lightly brush that thought to the side.

"I need you focused and ready tonight. We are trying something new."

Are we going back to Mount Taygetus?

"Not just yet. There are parts of the pattern that you need to witness before we return there. The energy patterns that Zeus set up with the Seven Sisters still affect your planet and people, even today."

She begins to raise her arm. Are you sending me off to the light already?

"This time will be quite different. Your energy is still connected to Zeus at this point; you can be there and here at the same time. I want to guide you through this experience."

Guide away!

"Oh, Ignomatius, I so wish you could see your energy the way I do. You have so much love in your heart."

I don't know how to respond.

"Don't respond, but do keep that heart connected to mine. I don't want your energy being suborned by Zeus."

An interesting choice of words…suborned?

"Watch and stay close to me."

You are coming along?

"All will be revealed, Ignomatius. All will be revealed."

I watch her raise her arm and as it rises, she takes my hand in hers. Together, we step into the Light.

***

We are standing near the edge of the secret cave where Zeus does his artwork. Zeus is intent upon his work. I look more closely and he is carving all of the Seven Sisters out of a small piece of rock. His control of lightning as a tool has substantially grown since last we saw him work. He is muttering to himself as he works. "Just a line here. One bit of light there. Add a blush of color to Maia's face. A blush on Maia's face. No. Stay focused. Add the life force energy from Maia. Now Electra. Now add…" He holds the piece up in the air to take a look at his progress.

Just as he raises his hand, Apollo and Orion pop into the cave unannounced. Apollo is speaking. "Zeus, old boy, what are you up to? We've been looking everywhere. What's…"

As Apollo's booming voice fills the cave, several things happen at once. Zeus, who is startled, throws his hands up in the air. The Hooded One makes a gesture and I feel a curtain of power fall between us and the gods. The statue of the Seven Sisters flies through the air and shatters as it hits Orion's armor. When it shatters, the sexual energy that Zeus had stored in the carving is released and fills the room. I watch as the three of them stand transfixed. The effect of the energy is pretty immediate and a bit beyond words. They were gods after all.

Apollo is the first to recover. "What was that? Zeus, you are holding out on us!"

Orion shakes himself. His eyes are still somewhat glazed. The smile on his face would light up the darkest night. "Wow! That was the best ever. I want more."

Zombielike, Orion moves toward the other statues in Zeus's collection. He is stopped immediately by a gesture from Zeus. Again, they stand transfixed. Orion and Zeus face each other. This time the strain in the room was palpable. Orion struggles to touch the statues. Zeus holds him standing in place, one god-like will pitted against another. It feels like they might shatter just as the statue had.

Apollo steps in between the two gods and breaks the energy just before it would snap. He holds Orion by the shoulders. "Get a grip, Orion. I am sure Zeus will explain to us what happened here."

Zeus spoke through clenched jaws. "I'll explain after we leave my sacred space. You are not welcome here again!"

It was so much more than just a pronouncement. I could feel the energy gather around Apollo and Orion, squeezing the space in which they stood. Then it felt like a pop with the sound of thunder ringing in my ears and we all stood on a mountain top. The Hooded One quickly gestured to reestablish a wall of energy between us and the towering gods. Towering and glowering, their energy was magnificent, and so dangerous. I could see how mortals were killed by a stray thought of these very gods.

Orion stood with his hands reaching towards Zeus, babbling now about need and want, energy and feminine power. More, more, more. Apollo finally shook him until the glazed-over look left Orion's eyes. Zeus took a deep breath and then adjusted his chiton. He gave Orion his best "I am about to smite you" glare.

Orion was unfazed, but he did seem to gain control of himself. "Zeus, old boy, what was that energy? I've never experienced anything quite like it while I have been in form."

Zeus stood and glared at Orion and Apollo. Once again, Apollo acted as peacemaker. "Zeus, we were looking for you and couldn't find you. I did a deep scan and found your energy hidden away in that cave. We were curious about what you were up to, so we just popped in. Then, wow, I have never experienced that kind of energy flux either. Not even the best ambrosia can touch that. Please tell us what happened there?"

Zeus, who was never immune to flattery, snorted and stamped his foot. I felt the mountain beneath us shake a bit and heard a small avalanche start down the mountain. I guess that anger had to go somewhere. I said a brief prayer that there wasn't a village in the path of the avalanche. When Zeus finally spoke, it sounded more like a confession than an explanation. "I have been doing some art work."

Orion started to giggle and Apollo stepped on his foot. "Zeus, those were some of the best statues of goddesses that I've ever seen. They were so lifelike. The detail was amazing."

Zeus blinked and then slowly smiled. "Do you think so?"

Apollo leaned closer. "You are truly talented. I am very impressed. How did you do that?"

Zeus was beaming. "Do you truly think I am talented?"

Apollo nodded and then poked Orion in the ribs. Orion chimed in.

"Those were the best goddesses I have ever seen. I mean statues. I mean statues of goddesses."

Apollo stepped on his foot again and Orion shut up. Zeus was totally transformed by their praise. He had kept his artwork hidden for so long, it was a relief to hear praise for something that he truly enjoyed doing. What did Hera and Athena know anyway? He almost got distracted by thinking about Hera, but Apollo cleared his throat.

Zeus continued. "I taught myself how to use my lightning abilities to carve rock into statues of Hera, but they just lacked something. Then I discovered how to focus my energy in a different way." Apollo and Orion were nodding encouragingly. "So Hera and I were doing sex magic one day," Zeus stopped briefly to glare again at Orion just in case he got ideas about Hera. Orion was still smiling vacuously so Zeus continued. "Because of the creative energy held within the womb, women hold a special connection to Source energy. I found a way to just nip a little bit of that energy during sex magic and then I use it in my art work."

Apollo interrupted. "What does Hera think about that?"

Zeus gave Apollo a laconic smile and said, "I didn't ask Hera what she thought about it. It's such a small amount of energy, she really didn't notice."

Apollo looked troubled. Orion couldn't contain himself. "So, Zeus, you are saying that the energy I felt when the statue broke was the release of pure Source energy you, um, cultivated during sex magic?"

Zeus nodded.

"You're amazing. Can you teach me how to do it? I have some artwork that I've been working on as well."

Zeus liked the word "cultivated". He felt a little less guilty. Maybe he would teach this young pup of a god how to do it.

The Hooded One gently touched my shoulder. I looked over at her. When I looked back the scene was fading and I could no longer hear the gods. They huddled close together, talking animatedly. The whole scene started fading away. Again, The Hooded One put her hand on my shoulder and we were back by the fire. I felt a little disoriented. It was so quiet and somehow confined.

"A sip of tea will help, Little One."

The tea was Bengal Spice tonight. Quite refreshing and comforting. I felt more in the here and now, as much as being with a mythical being was ever in the here and now. The Hooded One chuckled at my thoughts.

"You did quite well, Ignomatius."

So why were you there and what was that wall of energy?

"I was protecting you from being corrupted by the energy from the statues. You would have been just as dazzled as Orion if the energy hit you, even if you were in non-corporeal form. I'm afraid our work would have been over at that point. You would have stayed in a coma with your soul searching the universe for the Seven Sisters, just as Orion did."

So I guess it's just as well we didn't stay to hear how to do it? I must admit my question sounded wistful, even to my ear.

"Ignomatius, there are many things in the world of what you call magic that, just because you can do them, doesn't mean you should. What Zeus started sounded so innocent. The energetic pattern in humanity however has resulted in a great darkness in the human soul. Humans hunger for the love of Source more than anything else. Mostly it remains an unnamed yearning that they try to fill with so many of the distractions that come with form.

"The energy pattern created by Zeus was a very subtle, yet powerful, change in the male psyche. Instead of working in concert with feminine energy, men started trying to take or capture it, if you will, what remains one of the great mysteries in form: the creation of life force energy. It is a gift of Source held within the female womb that is sparked by the masculine

joining. That energy contains the essence of love or God, as most would call it."

So why can't we just connect with the love? The Hooded One leaned towards me and regarded me intensely. I felt my layers of defense peel away under that regard. I nearly squirmed in my seat. Perhaps now would be a good time to fall asleep, as in really asleep. She leaned back and I took a breath. I had stopped breathing.

"Little One, you are made of the love of God. It is your essence and the essence of everything in Form. Your heart yearns for something that is so intrinsically yours that there is no separating one from the other."

Then why don't I feel it? I mean, I have moments when I know what love is and it is such ecstasy, but it's like reaching for the ring on the merry-go-round. Every time I think I am close and that I will get it this time, I just miss it.

"It is the illusion of form. You already hold the ring and much, much more, but until you release yourself from the illusion, it will seem beyond your reach."

Release myself. That's absurd. I want this more than anything. Why would I block out God's love? It's not me. It's God. Why is He so absent, so far away that we must struggle and journey and thirst for the touch of God? The love of God? The Hooded One leaned towards me and gently touched my forehead.

"The barriers to God are only in here. God gives the magic of life. Then life is a journey back to God. Only God is never gone or lost, it is all an illusion."

You make it sound so simple.

"It is simple."

Then what is wrong with me? Why can't I find my way to God's love?

"Think of your greatest fear."

That I am not worthy of God's love. Not good enough. Not holy enough.

"The only thing that stands in the way of catching your ring is fear. The fear of not being enough; it is hard-wired into the human psyche. This is what you really struggle against; not God, not yourself, but the belief that you are not enough."

I've tried everything I know to do to change that. What more can I do?

"Choose love. Choose love every time you face that fear in whatever form it takes. The choice opens up a door to God and All That Is. Fear closes

the door and turns the key to lock it. The love you seek so desperately is always within you and around you. It is not an elusive quest that can never be finished."

It is so easy for you to say that. You are not stuck in form. The Hooded One pulled back from me.

"Perhaps you need a while to process this. There is more to explore with Zeus and the Seven Sisters. So much more than you even know, but your psyche must be ready for each step."

Abruptly she is gone and I am in my bed in the dark. I feel bereft. Finally I fall asleep. In my dreams I steal into Zeus's cave and take one of the statues. I just want to look at it. Zeus suddenly appears and I run through the night with Zeus hot on my trail, throwing bolts of lightning all around me.

***

It has been days since I last spoke with The Hooded One. It feels so much longer. I think of her often, but thoughts of her get all mixed up with thoughts of Zeus, Apollo, and Orion. In my dreams I am watching them from behind a curtain. They are talking so animatedly. I see Orion laugh and Apollo stamp his foot. Zeus is showing off his latest statue. Apollo glows as he tells his latest story. They are talking now to other gods. I try to reach beyond the curtain. "Tell Me! Tell me your stories." They hear me not. Part of me craves the wonders of their energy exploits, while part of me craves the quiet comfort of The Hooded One.

***

I have hiked up to the top of my favorite hills in a state game land about two hours from where I live. Perhaps here I can find some peace. The walk always helps me order my thoughts. Connecting with Nature helps me connect with the highest essence of my spirit. I hope it works for me today. I am in real need of that connection.

The river winds its way through the valley. There are railroad tracks on either side of the river. I hope no trains come through for a while as I try to focus inwardly. I focus on my breathing. Breathe in, slight hold. Breathe out. Slight hold.

As I move deeper into a meditative state, I see both Zeus and The Hooded One standing before me in my mind's eye. Zeus beckons me with a small vial that glows as he holds it out to me. My breathing stops. The Goddess essence. I am mesmerized by its light and the promise of energy such as I have never known. Just as I start to reach for it, I hear The Hooded One's voice. *"Choose love, Ignomatius."* It's such a quiet voice with a simple statement, but it rolls through me like thunder through the plains. Choose love. My hand comes back and I turn towards The Hooded One as though she is standing in front of me.

"Choose love. Open the door to that which you truly seek. It resides within you. Trust in that connection and you will never want again."

In my mind's eye, I see Zeus and the glowing vial start to fade away. I get up and turn to start my way back down the hill. A giant hawk flies right over my head and a bird starts a merry song in the tree next to me. My heart is light once again. With each step out of the forest, I choose love.

***

The Weaver paused her weaving. One of the strands suddenly pulsed with Light. She watched it flow back to the knotted node from Zeus and Electra. There was a little flash and one strand pulled loose from the knot. The Weaver smiled and proceeded on with her constant weaving. One with One with One, the strands melded into the pattern of wholeness.

Chapter Eight

"Only the veil of illusion separates you from that wholeness. Therein lies the crux of the human experience. Be ruled by the illusion or choose a path to wholeness." The Hooded One

The tea is especially good tonight, blueberry green tea with a hint of honey. I think the honey may have come from honeysuckle but I am no connoisseur of honey.

"All of the teas come from what your subconscious needs, Ignomatius."

Do you think I could do that in real life? Manifest the essentials that would satisfy my subconscious needs?

"The answer to that is one that most people find frustrating. You already create that which satisfies your needs, which shows up in your life in one form or another."

Oh please, my life would look so different if I was creating the solutions for all my needs.

"Until you confront and accept the patterns in your subconscious, they rule you in ways that confound the intellect. The beliefs of your two-year-old self show up in your life despite the maturity you have attained. At the same time, you are surrounded by all that you need to recognize your connection to Source or God/Goddess. Only the veil of illusion separates you from that wholeness. Therein lies the crux of the human experience. Be ruled by the illusion or choose a path to wholeness. For most people, it is the journey of several lifetimes."

I will have to think some more on this and process it. It doesn't seem to make sense. Why would my two-year-old self be in charge of my beliefs?

"The patterns of belief and experiences of learning to separate from your mother and father form the basis of the emotional and mental beliefs. Your mother and father become the stereotypes of god/goddess in the psyche. What the child perceives as a great threat can be a normal, everyday

experience for the adult, such as having a parent travel for work. The child feels abandoned and the lesson learned may be that the ones we love will abandon us. In the child's psyche, this translates into God will abandon us."

This is much deeper than I thought.

"Ponder it, Little One. Do some research. We can discuss it more once you have a handle on how the psyche recreates and draws the stereotypes of your childhood into your life. For now, I have a journey for you that will have a lot of drama. We still have many layers to reveal of the Sisters' story, just as you need to reveal the multiple dimensions of your psyche. But now, Zeus's psyche is at it again."

Zeus? Do you think I am ready to go near him again without getting caught up in wanting the elixir he peddles to the gods?

The Hooded One is raising her arm as she replies to me. *"You will be fine, Little One. On this issue, you have done your homework."*

And off I go into the light.

***

Sisyphus sat on the edge of the cliff and watched the ocean far below. He was practicing bi-location, the latest mystery that Merope had taught him. It was pretty cool to be on Oenopic Island and back at the castle at the same time. He could feel Merope touching his heart even when she wasn't here beside him. It was a little confusing to sort out two different sensory experiences simultaneously, which is why he was in an isolated place. It helped to not have too much stimulation.

As he watched the ocean, a dot appeared on the horizon. As it got closer, he was able to see a large eagle carrying a rather beautiful woman toward the island. Why would a bird be carrying a woman? Then it clicked. Zeus was approaching the island in his bird form and he was bringing company. Rather than end the bi-location experiment, Sisyphus hid behind a rock as Zeus quickly approached the very spot on which he had been sitting.

As they landed and Zeus took his human form, Sisyphus recognized the woman. It was Aegina, daughter of the river god, Asopus. Zeus was preparing to do sex magic with Aegina, who seemed to be quite taken by him. Sisyphus sighed quietly to himself. Maybe he would learn something as he watched Zeus do his magic, although he couldn't imagine there was much that Merope hadn't already revealed to him. He came close to exposing his presence as a deep sigh escaped his lips. Thinking about Merope strengthened his connection with her through his original form. Sisyphus had to focus on his breathing to stay in his body here on the island, even as his thoughts were taking him back to Merope. He was right about Zeus, though. Standard, ho-hum sex magic. Then Zeus did something that caught his eye; it was so appalling that he almost stepped out to stop him. Zeus was stealing life force energy from Aegina!

Sisyphus realized immediately that he was in no position to confront Zeus while he was bi-locating. He wasn't even sure he would confront Zeus when he was in his full strength. He was mortal after all. But he knew who could. In the blink of an eye, he was back in his own body. Before Merope could question him, he bi-located to Asopus.

"Asopus, Zeus is practicing sex magic with your daughter!"

Asopus blinked at him and then started laughing, "I hope she is having a good time."

"But I saw Zeus steal her life force energy without asking," Sisyphus retorted. He sent a picture of what he had seen into Asopus's mind. A wave of water washed over him as Asopus left to find Zeus. Sisyphus bi-located back to the island.

Asopus was already beating against the cliff's shore, roaring Zeus's name. Zeus looked down and laughed, but Asopus was not intimidated. The waves roared again and a stream of water hit Zeus in the chest. Zeus shot a bolt of lightning at Asopus. It dissipated through the ocean. Another bolt. Another stream. The gods raged at each other. Then a stream of water picked up Aegina off the rock and she disappeared, along with the raging water.

Zeus threw a few more bolts of lightning just to have the last word. Then he started stomping around and yelling in his big god voice. "Who told Asopus what I was doing?"

Sisyphus didn't mean to step out, but even he could not resist the power in Zeus's voice. "I did."

Zeus stopped mid-stride and stared at Sisyphus. "What do you mean, you did?"

Sisyphus straightened up. "I saw you steal life force energy from Aegina."

Zeus sputtered, "I wasn't stealing, I was cultivating."

Sisyphus couldn't hide the scorn from his voice. "Even the gods don't have the right to steal life force energy."

Zeus stamped his foot and the earth shook. "I am telling you, I didn't steal. I cultivated the energy." In his frustration at being caught, Zeus sent forth another bolt of lightning. Sisyphus sizzled and disappeared. Zeus stamped his foot again and growled. "At least that problem is handled."

***

I found myself abruptly back in the room with The Hooded One. The sound of lightning as it melted Sisyphus is still in my ears. Oh my goodness, Zeus killed Sisyphus!

"Zeus thought he killed Sisyphus. He killed his doppelganger. Such a trauma nearly did kill Sisyphus, but his form was being held by Merope. She did not let him die. Zeus and his cronies tried to kill Sisyphus a couple more times, but Merope and Sisyphus outsmarted them every time."

So doppelgangers are?

"It is possible to create a form that will project into another time and space with the full experience of the original body. It is one of the mysteries that were veiled from human consciousness."

Seems like it worked for Sisyphus.

"Indeed. So Sisyphus revealed Zeus's escapades with feminine energy. Orion kept chasing the Seven Sisters, just to get another taste, as he put it. They were not interested, but that didn't stop Orion from making a pest of himself."

So Zeus was an eagle when Sisyphus first saw him. He could change his shape?

"Shape shifters have a long history in human legends and, like all legends, they are based on stories with some factual basis. Zeus's specialty was not shape shifting, but it was the specialty of some of the Seven Sisters. That story is for our next time together. You've done enough traveling for this session. Get some rest and we'll see how it goes for the shape shifting."

I'll just shift into sleep so I get shaped up for the next session. The Hooded One smiles. It's taken her quite a while to appreciate my puns.

"Your puns need work. Shift that."

Ouch! I dream of words all night and try to pick the right one.

92

***

It's been several days since I've seen The Hooded One. Life has been hectic. It feels good to be next to the fire and sipping tea. Tonight, it's a good, strong, Scottish tea with lots of cream and sugar, as usual. I look askance at The Hooded One and she responds.

"You will need your energy tonight, Ignomatius, for you are off to witness the mating of Zeus and Taygeta."

Mating? An odd choice of words.

"Their son, Lacedaemon, founded Sparta. Do you remember Taygeta's mental discipline as she came into the world?"

I nod as I see mathematical equations dancing in the flames of the fire. It feels like Taygeta is standing next to me.

"That discipline was one of her many gifts to her beloved land. She was an exacting goddess and not a very tolerant one, but her love of the wild coast and the mountains around her tempered her energy somewhat. The nature of her energy was expressed through the peoples of Sparta."

They were so disciplined. Their military skills have never been matched.

"Taygeta's innate energy is the reason she and Artemis got along so well. They were the best of friends."

So why are we bringing up Artemis?

"You will see."

The Hooded One is raising her arm as she speaks. I go joyfully into the light to see my friend, Taygeta.

***

Artemis and Taygeta are sitting together and finishing off the remnants of two hares. They have been hunting together and lunch was quite tasty. The view down the mountain is spectacular, worthy of the two goddesses who are enjoying the scenery, along with their lunch.

Artemis is talking quite animatedly to Taygeta. "I so enjoy hunting in your woods. The terrain here is so delightfully rugged that it lends an enticing challenge to the hunt."

I watch them laugh and talk for a while. It's much like any two friends out for lunch. Then suddenly their whole demeanor changes. Taygeta looks around the area as if she is ready to go on the hunt again. She speaks to Artemis softly in her, "I don't want to spook the prey" voice.

"He's here. I can feel him. I know it's time, but Zeus has made us all so mad with stealing energy that way. I need him for my offspring, but I must find a way to avoid his little 'cultivating' trick as he calls it."

Artemis looks thoughtfully at the magnificent hinds hitched to her chariot. They were a deeper red than wild female red deer and their hides glistened like they had been attended by the best stable hand. They were much more muscular than normal deer as well. She looks at Taygeta in that same thoughtful manner and then speaks. "Why don't you shape shift into a hind like one of mine over there. We are close enough that you can easily imprint their form. If we keep Zeus running, he won't have time to absorb the form fully and he'll have to stay focused on his shape shifting. That way he won't be able to take any energy because he will lose the form."

Taygeta looks thoughtfully at the hinds as well. "That certainly would add an interesting mix to the energy. Your hinds are so unique."

Artemis smiles at her compliment. They both know how hard she had worked to breed the hinds that drew her carriage. The hinds were an essential part of her hunting expeditions. Their intelligence and ability to communicate were extraordinary.

Then to my complete surprise, Taygeta looked right at me as she said to Artemis, "Anchor Ignomatius's energy during the chase so that the observation doesn't get interrupted."

Artemis nods and then, before I can even catch a breath, Taygeta turns into the most beautiful hind right before my eyes. She is about three hands higher than Artemis's hinds with a set of the most gorgeous golden horns atop her head. Zeus pops into the campsite. Taygeta looks at him and then runs off into the woods. Zeus grins and not to be outdone, turns into a towering stag with a very impressive set of antlers. He takes off after Taygeta in the blink of an eye.

I'm left gaping at Artemis. She gets up and strolls over to her chariot and climbs in. As she grabs the reins, she turns toward me and says, "If you want to witness this, come along now." I find myself on the chariot and off she goes after Zeus and Taygeta.

I have seen movies where the camera sits on the front of the chase car and you have this careening view of the wildest chase scene. That's exactly what was happening. It was like I was plastered to the front of the chariot and racing through the most rugged terrain at 90 miles an hour. It was one of the most thrilling and yet chilling experiences of my life.

Who could drive a chariot through virgin woods at 90 miles an hour? Artemis! Magically, we would squeeze through the narrow passages, fly over the large boulders and cross streams without sinking into their waters. She managed to maneuver on the narrowest deer paths through the woods like they were a four-lane highway. I finally remembered to breathe, but I am pretty sure I was close to passing out from complete oxygen deprivation.

By the time we caught up to Zeus and Taygeta, they were already starting the sex magic ritual. Zeus was definitely sweating and trying not to show the effects of the chase through the woods while maintaining his form. It was obvious that Taygeta was in the lead, as she invoked the raw spirit of the land to protect and sanctify the small glen.

Silently, Artemis had slowed her chariot to a spot where she could observe but not be observed, putting her hunting skills to good use. I still wasn't sure if she had squeezed through the trees or if the forest had moved to accommodate her passage. I was very glad to be back to my regular disembodied state.

As I watched Taygeta invoking the energies, I saw Artemis add her own into the mix. Artemis, warrior and protector of her friend, Taygeta, held the energy within the circle for the sanctity of the working. Zeus would not be cultivating Taygeta's energy on this day. How interesting that the conception of Lacedaemon, son of Taygeta and founder of Sparta, held the energy of this triunity. Taygeta brought to the working her clear, disciplined mind. Artemis added her warrior/protector spirit. Zeus, with his passion flowing like the rain of a heavy storm, wove into the pattern his fiery temper, contained and mastered by the channels of Taygeta's spirit.

They were through all the motions of the ritual before Zeus even had time to think. By the time he thought about taking a little bit of Taygeta's energy, it was too late. By the gods, he was Zeus and he would have some of her energy for his collection. In his stag form, he snorted challenge and stamped his foot. In an instant, Artemis stood between Zeus and Taygeta with her bow and arrow drawn and aimed at Zeus's heart. Zeus dropped the form of the stag. He briefly looked like he might try to smite Artemis, but even Zeus wasn't about to challenge The Warrior Queen. He stamped his foot in frustration and disappeared from the glen.

Taygeta emerged from her form, but the carcass, replete with the golden horns, remained upon the forest floor. She solemnly picked it up and held it out to Artemis. "A sacrifice for your protection, my friend."

Artemis accepted the carcass and just as solemnly took it over to her chariot and laid it over the side. Then she turned back to Taygeta and they gazed at each other for one long moment. I think their Goddess voices filled the whole land as they laughed and hugged.

"Did you see his face?"

"That was too perfect!"

"You certainly gave him quite the chase."

"Well, I had to wear him out."

"Do we have our boy?"

"Yes! I can feel him growing already!"

"We will teach him how to hunt."

"We will teach him how to do math."

They both paused a moment. Their joyous laughter filled the glen again.

Chapter Nine

"Most humans do not know what love is or believe in its power. They do not believe in themselves either. It is all the same. The illusion of being in this world is generated by and pierced by the power of love."
The Hooded One

The Hooded One seems a little agitated tonight as we sit in silence. I pause as I sip my tea and look at her. I have never seen her like this before. What's up?

She does not respond and sits silently. It feels like she is wringing her hands. At last, she speaks.

"Ignomatius, it is time to send you on a journey that I am not sure you are ready for. I hesitate to do this, for I cannot protect you on this journey, you will have to protect yourself."

Chills run down my spine as she speaks. I've been through some rather "interesting" experiences with The Hooded One and she has always protected me from harm. What could possibly be more dangerous than being besotted like Orion?

"I am sending you off to visit Celaeno."

Why would that be dangerous? There is nothing in the legend that suggests anything dangerous about her.

"Celaeno was a master at manipulating human DNA. She experimented for centuries to achieve a human hybrid that would live longer, as well as exhibit some of the more esoteric traits of the Immortals."

What type of esoteric traits?

"Telepathy, teleportation, shape shifting and so on."

You mean all the very interesting traits that we yearn for as part of our spiritual evolution?

"You yearn for what truly belongs to you already. You are as much a part of the Divine Matrix as any of the Immortals. The potential exists within your DNA structure for much more than what humanity limits itself to."

And exactly what is the dangerous part of this?

"When I mentioned human hybrids, the hybrid part was most often not human DNA. Celaeno mixed in animal DNA along with Immortal DNA. Unlike Zeus, who spread his DNA through sacred sex, Celaeno grafted genetic codes, much like the crude attempts at genetic manipulation in current times; only her work was light years beyond what your scientists know at this time. Entire legends exist around her cadre of hybrids."

Legends?

"Werewolves, vampires, chimeras. Her line of work remained hidden, even from other Immortals at the time."

So this is dangerous because I am walking into a den of werewolves and vampires?

"Well, not so much that, even though they will be able to sense you. It's more that Celaeno will want your DNA because of your ability to travel through time."

Then why don't you come along and shield me like you did with Zeus?

"Celaeno wants my DNA as well, and she must not have it. She will try to get it through you."

How can you have DNA when you are not real? I mean physical. I mean you don't have a body.

"She is capable of pulling DNA structures even from that which is etheric energy. DNA is the physical code of your etheric body and abilities, it is patterned with possibilities based upon your soul projection and purpose in this lifetime. DNA connects directly into your interdimensional being and reflects portions of that being into form."

So you do have a body of sorts?

"Oh, Ignomatius, being with you is as close to being in form as I get. By my assuming a form within your consciousness, it has set up a genetic pattern that resonates with your genetic pattern. It is part of the energetic connection that enables us to communicate with each other."

Why shouldn't your DNA be used by Celaeno? What harm is there in adding your incredible, wonderful self into the human DNA pool?

"We are talking about hybrids with psychic potentials and long lives. Think about this. You travel through time and I open the portals. Humanity's ability to manipulate time was limited for a reason and purpose within the great Plan of Source. The combination of our work within a hybrid would create a potential being that your world is just not ready for."

I am stunned by her words. I have always been intrigued and honored by our work together, but I have never thought of it in terms The Hooded One has just expressed. I was so wrapped up in my own spiritual journey and growth that the greater implications escaped me. Time manipulation? Why me?

"Why you, indeed. That is a question, Ignomatius, which you must ask yourself, for the answer lies within. When you can see who and what you are, the answer will be there."

I need to ponder that over several more cups of tea. I feel her answering smile. It sounds like Celaeno is almost evil. How can she be one of the Seven Sisters and create monsters?

"Firstly, her creations were not monsters. Most of the lore around the hybrids is a combination of fantasy and fear. Secondly, humanity is not the only species evolving upon this planet. Your arrogance and fear cloud your perceptions of what other species are capable of in this realm. Thirdly, remember that humanity is a reflection of Source. Your species is on the verge of an evolutionary leap. The work of Celaeno had much to do with the genetic combinations that will enable that leap to occur. Lastly, Celaeno is the most loving and kind of all the sisters. That is the true danger for you. Her essential sweetness and softness will lure you in to the point where there is no escape. The emanations of love are so strong around her that she literally had to stay hidden to not affect humanity in ways that humanity was not prepared for."

So how do I protect myself from Celaeno's energy?

"I do not have an answer for that. Love is. You are. I will give you a mantra that might help, but it is meant to dispel fear and doubt. Repeat this: greater is that which is within me, than that which is within the world."

Greater is that which is within me, than that which is within the world.

"There is great power in this statement. It takes you to your true connection to Source, as it grounds you in your power in the moment."

It sounds nice, but I don't get it. How will this protect me? I have used mantras to get into a meditative state. Meditation won't protect me from werewolves or a master DNA manipulator.

The Hooded One leans in close to my face. She has never been this close before. *"Love is its own protection. When you are in a state of love, no harm will come to you."*

My body reverberates with the power of her words as though I am standing in a bell tower when the bells were ringing. She leans back and I take a breath as she continues.

"When you have mastered that statement, they could drop a nuclear bomb next to you and you would not come to harm. Love is that powerful in its pure state. Most humans do not know what love is or believe in its power. They do not believe in themselves either. It is all the same. The illusion of being in this world is generated by and pierced by the power of love."

I take a deep breath and as I start to speak she raises her finger to stop me.

"Do not joke here. Do not belittle your power. Do not demean love. Take some time and work with the mantra. Then we will see about sending you on your next journey."

Abruptly, I wake up in my bed. It is cold and dark and I am alone. I shiver even under the quilt. I hear The Hooded One's voice.

"Greater is that..."

I finish the mantra in my head, repeating it over and over again, hoping that somehow the repetition will make it real to me. I drift back to sleep. My dreams are about werewolves and vampires chasing me. I keep trying to remember in my dream what I need to do. When I finally remember the mantra and say it, the monsters are gone and I go into a deep, dreamless sleep.

***

It's been a couple of weeks since I last saw The Hooded One. I've had several opportunities to use the mantra. It seems to help sometimes. I was driving in a heavy rain and the car started fishtailing. I remembered to say the mantra. "Greater is that which is within me..." Immediately, my fear was gone and the road conditions were better. It seemed so synchronistic at the time. My dreams are still full of monsters. When I can remember the mantra, it helps, but I am tired from being chased night after night.

I ponder The Hooded One's words about love. I have moments when I can see and feel love as she describes it and embodies it. Being in her energy as she speaks of love is probably the most powerful part for me. I can feel it in my bones when I am with her, but that sense of wonder and joy seems to fade away as I go through my daily life. How can I maintain it?

"Feed it with your thoughts, choices, and actions, Little One."

It's always about choice, isn't it?

"You've been taught by your culture to feed that which belittles you and your power. Choose to feed love."

Thank you, my friend.

"Thank you. Come and visit me tonight. I think you are ready for your next journey."

***

A strong, black tea with lots of cream and sugar awaits me when I come sit by the fire.

"I want you on your toes tonight, Little One. Here's a good cup of tea to fortify you for your journey."

You are sending me off with a cup of tea instead of some kind of protective talisman?

"There's a lot of love in that tea and..."

Love is its own protection. I know. Well, it's a perfect cup of tea, but I would prefer to have a little something more between me and a werewolf.

"You will have Celaeno between you and the werewolf. He is her son, after all. Be aware. Now drink up. It's time."

I drink down the tea once it has cooled. When I look up The Hooded One is raising her arm, but I feel a cautionary note in her energy.

"Remember, Ignomatius, no DNA transfers."

I've left my DNA at home, I quip as I step into the light.

***

Something must have gone wrong. I am sitting at the table with The Hooded One and there is a cup of tea in front of me. The tea has the most wonderful aroma. The Hooded One gestures toward the tea to encourage me to take a sip. I reach toward the tea. My hand stops short of the cup. Something is wrong here. Everything looks like the cozy room where I meet with The Hooded One, but it is not her presence within the hooded cowl that faces me. Not her presence at all.

The scene shifts abruptly. I am standing on a path. It is an amazingly beautiful day and I am surrounded by the lush wonder of early Greece. My senses are overwhelmed by the pure sensual perfection of it all. There is a woman walking down the path ahead of me. I seem to know her. Celaeno! I rush down the path to catch up with her. She hurries away from me as I get close. Just as I am about to catch up with her, she veers off the path and goes through a gate. The gate slams shut behind her. I reach for the gate to follow her. My hand stops short of the latch. Touch transfers DNA, I've learned from watching crime shows on TV. This is a trick. The scene shifts.

I gasp as I nearly fall off a narrow path along a steep cliff. I lean my weight toward the cliff wall and close my eyes to give myself a moment to get oriented. When I open them, I see a woman walking slowly down the ledge before me. Celaeno, again. I approach more cautiously this time, but she doesn't seem to be hurrying away. She seems a little tipsy. As I get closer, I can hear her labored breathing. Is something wrong with her? Is she ill? I hurry to catch up. Just as I am a few paces away, she falls over the edge of the path. Oh my goodness! I rush to the place she fell and look down the steep cliff. Celaeno is hanging precariously by one hand and about to fall to her death. The most beautiful eyes I have ever seen are staring up at me, scared and pleading. I hear her melodic, quavering voice for the first time. "Help me! Please help me!"

I reach to grasp her hand. It feels like time has stopped. It takes an eternity for my hand to traverse the short distance to her hand. I stop just shy of her hand. For the first time, I feel the unconditional love that I experience from The Hooded One flowing through me. I am so much love. I note the shift in Celaeno's eyes as she registers what I am experiencing. A tender smile is on my lips as I withdraw my hand. The scene shifts.

The next scene is so incongruous that it takes me several minutes to process what I am seeing. We are in a cottage somewhere. More than a cottage. A grand villa with a breathtaking garden filling my view of the window. Celaeno is sitting at a table with two others with what is obviously the remains of breakfast spread casually between the three of them. Her beauty and melodic voice fills the space. Like the other sisters, her presence is an elemental force that touches and overwhelms the very fibers of my being. Added to that, my mind slowly processes what I am seeing into an understandable tableau: the two other beings having breakfast with her are not quite human. One being is dark and brooding. His energy shifts and I feel an ancient awareness of deep animal connection to the earth. His face resembles a wolf as he connects with that energy. For a brief moment, I see man and wolf as one being. It is very disorienting.

I turn my attention to the other being that looks quite extraordinary. He has the head of a man, the torso of a lion, and the legs of a goat, with his tail ending with a snake head. His energy is so gentle and kind. He seems so vulnerable sitting there, which makes me feel protective. As I have that thought, a flash of energy goes from the wolf man around the chimera that has the same protective feel. The elder brother protecting his younger, fragile brother. I am witnessing Celaeno having breakfast with her two sons, Lycus and Chimaerus. Now that I have my perspective straight, I can actually follow the conversation.

Chimaerus is speaking earnestly to his mother. "Mother, I know you want me to venture out into the world, but I can't hide who and what I am, like Lycus. People will stare. I can't stand it."

Celaeno leans toward him and I feel her mother's love wrap around him. "You are so sensitive. That sensitivity is a gift that is part of your abilities. I have kept you here to protect you until you have matured. The next stage is to go out into the world and learn to function. Perhaps I should have exposed you more to the world as you were growing up to make this easier."

Lycus interrupts, "You will have me by your side. No harm will come to you."

Chimaerus pales as the force of Lycus's words wash over him. "See, Mother, even my own brother assails my shields with the force of his personality. How will I be able to function around humans?"

Celaeno reaches out to touch Chimaerus. "My dear son, I have given you all the tools you need to function in this world. You only need to practice. It will come easier with exposure to humanity over time. You were never meant to live like a monk on a mountain. Besides, Electra needs you both to complete her working at Dardanus."

A shock goes through me at the mention of Electra.

Lycus has a laconic smile on his face. His deep voice practically purrs as he says, "I am so looking forward to helping Electra."

Chimaerus's voice squeaks as he says, "I'm not sure I am ready to participate in the Rites of Demeter."

Celaeno smiles at them both. The room is electric with young male sexual tension. "Chimaerus, you are still a virgin for a reason. You will sacrifice your virginity on the altar. When it is time, you will be ready, my shy one."

Lycus snorts with laughter and slaps Chimaerus on the shoulder. "I will be there to guard you as well, my dainty brother."

What is Electra doing in Dardanus? I hope she is not getting into more trouble. As I turn my attention away from the scene before me, it fades.

***

I am standing among the stars. The Hooded One is next to me. I know that it is really her this time, even though this is not how we usually connect.

"We can communicate without pulling you from your journey and be shielded from Celaeno's attention. How are you doing, Little One?"

Well, I think I am okay. There has been a lot of shifting and change in venue. Celaeno seems to know when I am around except for this last time.

"She knew you were witnessing that scene. It was one of her favorite moments. Spending time with her sons was very precious to her. They were the culmination of a lot of work."

So how is Electra involved in this?

"Electra's son, Dardanus, founded what is known today as Troy. Electra's work to change the path of humanity did not stop with her fall from Olympus. She tried working with humans directly, a lot like Merope and Sisyphus. You will be visiting her again."

I don't quite understand what to do with Celaeno. She's been trying to sample my DNA, but so far I have managed to avoid it.

"You are doing well, Ignomatius. I am just giving your energy a break."

As she speaks, she reaches up and touches the starry void that surrounds us. A trail of light travels down her arm. She reaches out the other arm to lightly touch my heart and the starlight circles around me briefly and then goes back to the stars. What was that?

"I just reenergized your being with a reminder that it is light. Light feeds you on so many levels. It also added energy to your protective aura."

Thanks, but I think I am doing well with Celaeno.

"Remember that Celaeno is a force of the stars in human form. So are you, Ignomatius. So are you."

She raises her arm and off I go into the light, fortified with who knows what from the stars.

***

Celaeno is sitting on a bench in her garden, looking at the stars. There is a note of envy in her voice as she speaks to me. "So, our little time traveler friend, what's it like to work with The Hooded One?"

The Hooded One is mysterious and kind. I think of my recent experience with her. She is amazing beyond words.

Celaeno's voice darkens like the night around her as she replies. "As am I, Ignomatius. Do not forget that."

I bow my head in acknowledgement of the power of the most recent one of the Seven Sisters that I have had the privilege to meet. It is an honor and a joy. As her energy brightens in response to my homage, I sense a darker shadow behind her, a presence tainted with secrets. It disappears into the night before I can process anything more about it. Celaeno quickly draws my attention back to her. "I have children, not of my blood, who visit me from time to time. It's best if you don't connect with their energy." She pats the bench next to her. "Come and sit next to me."

I slowly walk over to take a seat on the bench across from her. I stop just before I sit down. Another ploy. I need to be on my guard. Celaeno sighs. The night around us sighs with her. Abruptly, we are back in the kitchen. I am a little startled.

Celaeno smiles at me. "Sorry, I just felt like a cup of ginger tea before bed. Would you like one?" I shake my head and she chuckles.

"A little too obvious, but truly, despite what The Hooded One may have told you, my genetic manipulations are for the good of humanity. Gene lines are manipulated all the time. Surely, you know that."

I have a brief image of my mother introducing me to her latest idea of a good mate for me. Oh yes, genetic lines are always manipulated.

Celaeno continues her friendly chatter with me. "It's too bad you can't meet some of my other fascinating creations. Most of them did not walk openly amongst humans. Many of them made history as legends. Humans tend to be afraid of that which is different. You are very different, but it is not obvious to those around you. I really need only a small sample to preserve your uniqueness for all time. It's not likely that you will mate. I have a small gift of foretelling someone's future. You could have a future here."

As she speaks, she is getting closer to me. I take a step back. Her voice is very enticing as she continues. "Come, Ignomatius. I am not scary like Zeus or his cronies. I assure you that I will only use your DNA for the highest good of all." She smiles her most beautiful goddess smile. I feel my defenses softening from her loving assault on my resolve.

Celaeno brightens even more as I have that thought. "You are welcome to visit here more often so that you may become more comfortable with my work. I would love to get to know you better."

She steps closer. I step back. There is not all that far to go in the kitchen. I am almost against the wall. Celaeno continues her assault, for I feel assaulted even with her loving eyes and loving words. She wants my DNA and she will do whatever it takes to get it. I am starting to feel penned in as she steps closer. In my panic, I blurt out, "You cannot have my DNA!"

Her eyes change. They are no longer human. Her breath roughens and I feel her exhale heating up the space around me. The hair on the back of my neck is standing up. In this very small kitchen, I am suddenly face to face with a rather large dragon. I feel like I am facing a towering tsunami with the certain knowledge that I am about to die.

She speaks. "I can and I will have a sample of your DNA. I have been polite. I do not need to ask. Just because you are too small to understand the importance of my work does not mean you get to impede it with your tiny will. Give me a sample of your DNA!!!"

Her command changes the very molecules in the air around me. As I stand face to face and eye to eye with a real live dragon who is about to do whatever it is that dragons do their victims, I have only one thought. "Greater is that which is within me than that which is within the world." It is so curious. With that thought, I am filled with such a sense of peace. There is not one iota of fear within me. I face the dragon and say, "I do have a choice. You may not have a sample of my DNA!"

The dragon disappears and Celaeno is in her human form once more. She seems to be distressed as she turns around looking at the many herbs on her kitchen shelves. She faces me with her eyes downcast and speaks again. "I am so sorry. In my pursuit of perfection, I overstepped the boundaries of what is love. I tried to take away your free will. I am so sorry. I....I..."

And she disappears from the kitchen. I am stunned. I step out of the kitchen and back into the garden to see if she is there. She is not. Instead, I face a very angry Lycus. At this point, he is half human and half wolf. His growl is echoed in the darkness by several other voices. I am surrounded by werewolves.

"What did you do to my mother, Ignomatius?" I feel him lean in close to me. "Yes, I can sense your energy even if you are not in form. My abilities as a wolf extend beyond the physical. You will not leave here unless I let you."

I feel a psychic wall of energy surround me from the circle of wolves in the darkness. I am trapped, even though I have no body in this place.

Lycus growls again and his words form in my head. "No one upsets my mother and lives. You die tonight."

I wish I could say that I had the same inner peace facing the werewolves that I did with the dragon. I did not. I was petrified and knew I was about to die. The primal fear of being faced with ancient, bestial, brute force overwhelmed my spiritual sense of self. Celaeno would, at last, get her sample of my DNA in the bloody shreds of my soul left from the assault of this pack of werewolves.

Suddenly, I felt a hint of that dark energy that had been in the garden with Celaeno earlier. It touched my mind with a questing, curious touch.

With an even deeper growl, the wolf pack stopped facing me and faced looking out. Lycus was in full wolf form now and his hackles were raised. He was so enormous. I caught a brief thought from leader to the pack. "Vampire! To the hunt!"

They all disappeared into the night. I tried breathing. It felt good. Now would be a good time to wake up in my bed.

***

With that thought, I was there. I bunched the covers around me protectively. In my own little corner, in my own little bed. Safe at last.

The Hooded One appeared at the bottom of my bed. How odd. She had never appeared in my world before. Her voice filled the room and its sound soothed my ruffled soul.

"Little One, you are close enough to the sleep state that I can connect on the visual level with your energy. Your energy is still highly charged from your recent experience. I can use that to strengthen our bond."

As you wish. It is so good to see you.

"It is good to see you as well. You did well tonight."

I am just glad to be alive.

"I'm glad you are alive as well. More than you know."

The smile in her voice washes over me and softens the battered edges of my psyche. It was a rough journey. Werewolves. Dragons. Vampires.

"Go back to sleep, Little One. I will stand guard for the rest of the night. No harm will come to you in your dreams."

My eyes were drooping into sleep as she spoke. My last sight was of The Hooded One standing guard in my bedroom as I slept a long, dreamless sleep.

Chapter Ten

"It truly is thought and intent that create change on the physical plane. When your scientists can measure the effects of thought, magic will be considered science once again."   The Hooded One

I awoke the next morning with pain in all my joints feeling very grouchy. The Hooded One has explained to me that it's an after effect of the energy work. My physical form resists absorbing the energy from my journeys and reacts negatively. I hear the echo of The Hooded One's voice saying, "Love is its own protection" and "Greater is that which is within me than that which is within the world."

I try breathing into the pain and releasing it. Breathing helps some, but not much. My memory flashes back to standing among the stars; perhaps if I embrace and try to accept the energy, it will help. My breathing gets slower and deeper as I remember the events of the previous night. As I feel my resistance, I invite it into my heart and acknowledge the depth of my experience.

Suddenly, it feels like I am floating on the waves of the ocean. The pain from my joints washes toward me and I float on top of it as it floats away. I invite the light of the stars into my heart and remember the joy and wonder of that moment. I finish the meditation with more breathing and stretches.

At the same time as I am dealing with the pain, I am swimming in light from being in the stars with The Hooded One last night. While it is an interesting phenomenon, I don't particularly want a repeat of my experience after Zeus and Maia. I go through some Tai Chi moves and focus on each part of my body as it performs the gentle movements. By the time I am done, I am grounded in the here and now and my pain and grouchiness are gone. Perhaps some lemon tea would be a good start for breakfast. I definitely don't need any caffeine this morning.

The image of The Hooded One standing guard at the bottom of my bed flashes through my mind. What a journey I am on! The day remains full of joy and wonder as I go through my simple chores and errands.

***

I am sitting with The Hooded One and we have been discussing my last journey. My experience with Celaeno has changed my whole perspective of what is real. I keep looking at people in the crowds around me and wonder if someone I see is not human. How much have other races merged into our "normal" human experience? Do dragons walk among us? The Hooded One smiles at my thoughts.

"Many of the races, such as the dragons or the elves, shifted into other dimensions rather than stay on the Earth plane through the Dark Times. As humanity developed their gifts of logic and reason, much of the awareness of what you would call magic was lost or outright discouraged for most of mankind. People who retained their awareness and connection were feared, ostracized, and persecuted."

So magic truly has been lost? Even I can hear the wistfulness in my voice.

"What you call magic is the science of other dimensions. Your scientists are just getting to the point where they can measure the science of energy manipulation. It looks like magic to most people. The Seven Sisters were all masters of that science. It truly is thought and intent that create change on the physical plane. When your scientists can measure the effects of thought, magic will be considered science once again."

So Celaeno was the mad scientist of the Seven Sisters?

"Oh, dear Ignomatius, it's hard for you to comprehend the true genius of Celaeno's work. There are centuries of fear, prejudice, and misinformation between now and the millennia in which Celaeno actively functioned on your plane. Celaeno's work with genetic lines was much like Electra's work with the threads of light. Genetically, the human race is designed to function at high levels of spiritual connection. The stories of humans living long lives, such as Noah and The Ark, have a great deal of truth to them. Humanity is on the brink of realizing the amazing potential that resides within the genetic codes transmitted through the ages."

What releases that potential within us?

"Embracing Oneness with the All. Releasing age old beliefs and limitations. Choosing love instead of fear. The answers sound simplistic. The power of these answers will be revealed as the vibrational nature of your world and species evolve."

Then I should search out the werewolves and vampires in this age and embrace them?

"If your work involves other species, they will find you. I would recommend that you don't look too hard for vampires. Your energy pattern was noticed by that vampire who was visiting Celaeno. Hopefully, that connection has faded over the ages."

Are there really vampires, then?

"Let it go, Ignomatius. Focus on the work we are doing now."

So where to next?

"Alcyone. Are you familiar with her story?"

She was petitioned by sailors to soothe the storms.

"One of the many versions of her stories. Have you studied the astrological impact of the Pleiades?"

No, not much.

"The star, Alcyone, is considered to be the center of your galaxy. Perhaps her story is a little more than directing storms out of the path of sailing ships."

The Hooded One's arm starts to rise. Off I go into the light, ready or not for the stormy energy of Alcyone.

***

Once again, I find myself in an alien environment and it takes me a few minutes to get oriented. This time I am in water, probably the ocean. There is a humongous creature swimming in front of me. Not a whale, perhaps a squid or an octopus. I feel the awareness of the creature's focus on me. It's not a comfortable feeling. The creature is reading my thoughts.

"Comfort, Ignomatius? Is that what you truly want?"

I am here to observe, not petition. Are you Alcyone?

"This is one of my many forms. I enjoy the waters. This form holds my energy much more easily than my human form."

Then you can be human as well?

"I am human simultaneously, as well as many expressions of Source in form. Human is not my favorite; it has so many limitations. Would you like to see my true nature?

111

Yes, I think so. Suddenly the creature turns and I am facing a giant maw; a giant maw that is sucking me in. What have I gotten myself into?

Instead of finding myself being devoured by a giant digestive system, I am moving rapidly through the stars. It's like being on ultra-fast forward. Stars are coming at me and speeding by before I can even register what is happening. As I fly, my energy is expanding, larger and larger. I am a star! Just as I think that, a large star appears in front of me and I collide, one star into another. There is light. More light. More and more light.

***

I come to slowly. My senses have been overwhelmed. I have a sense of lying on something, perhaps a bed. I reach and feel my hand moving through the air. I breathe and it's the purest, cleanest air I have ever inhaled. I am afraid to open my eyes, if I still have eyes to open.

"Ignomatius, do not try to impose your human experience on where you are right now."

I hear Alcyone's voice. I must have ears. Where am I?

"You are within my consciousness."

What does that mean?

"Don't try to define this experience. Just be!"

Her voice reverberates through me, "Just be." What does that mean? To just be?

"Let go of thought. Let go of needing to hold form."

Who would I be without my form?

"Light, Ignomatius, light."

I am Light …

***

Again, I come to. How long was I in a state of being light? Where am I now? I feel a breeze blowing on my face, smell flowers, and hear the sweet sound of birds near me. I open my eyes. This time I do have eyes. Alcyone is standing in front of me, looking out over the lush landscape of ancient Greece. Her face is lit by the sunlight with the breeze blowing through her dark hair. Her

112

expression seems sad, unlike the joy held in the countenances of the other sisters. She turns toward me. It is hard to stay grounded. I want to go back to being light. She speaks with the voice of the land around us. The sound is filled with the song of the birds, the colors of the flowers, the light of the sun and the deep foamy earth beneath us.

"Why would I want to be human when I am Light? Why limit myself?"

I have no answer. I am still bewildered by my experience.

"You cannot answer for me. I have shared with you the nature of our being that you might begin to understand that which I am. The fullness of my being lies beyond human understanding."

I look upon the depth of emotion in her face as she gazes into the valley. What is there that affects her so?

"Below us is the valley of Boeticia. Hyrineus, my son, is king there. My daughter dwells there as well. I did not spend much time in form as their mother. Humans are more valued by their father, Poseidon, than by me. I look at my sisters' children and wonder if I have missed something by not participating in their lives. You have met several of my sisters' offspring. What do you think?"

Again, I am silent. I have no answer. She turns toward me and her face is all light. Light streams from her body.

"The energy which I hold cannot be contained within the human form. That which I would give my children would destroy them, so they feel emptiness where they should have their mother's connection and turn to Zeus or Apollo or Poseidon for sustenance. The masculine energy of the gods feeds them, but does not replace the true substance of the Mother. They and their children will search through time for what I cannot give until they find it within themselves."

Humanity is still searching for its mother connection. I stand beside her with that yearning within my heart, the yearning to be touched by the light of love and know the wholeness of love.

Again she speaks, but her body is disappearing into the light as her voice continues on. "My energy is at the center of the universe. We came to the Earth Plane to witness the magnificent creation of Gaia, Mother to the Earth. The mother connection is a part of all creation. It is a part of your wholeness. Be in wholeness and you will find that which you seek."

As she speaks, I feel myself expanding. I am in space and witnessing Gaia, the goddess energy that birthed the earth, encompassing a rock in space. The rock becomes the blue planet of Earth. Water forms in the basins. Wind from the breath of creation patterns the earth as air comes into being. Lightning hurls through the sky. Life force energy lurks in the primal soup of the elemental matrix and takes shape as creatures of the water, air, and land.

I feel a touch upon my shoulder. I turn around as I move through the stars and The Hooded One is standing next to me.

"Come, Ignomatius, before you get lost in the story of creation."

I see The Hooded One briefly nod acquiescence to Alcyone and the scene before me disappears. For a moment, I am back on Mount Taygeta leaning against the pyramid that formed from Taygeta's emergence into form. Then I am in Celaeno's kitchen, Zeus's den, and Merope's ritual room. I see Electra with lines of energy around her. Maia's cave is before me and I dive into the darkness of the earth. I emerge in the cozy room with The Hooded One sitting opposite me. Why does she seem a little piqued with me after that amazing journey?

"Oh, Ignomatius, it's just that I don't quite know what to do with you. Your energy is much too big right now to send you off to your bed."

How about a cup of ginger tea then?

At first my reply catches her off guard and then we both laugh. I can feel the laughter reverberating through the many dimensions of light. Then a sip of pungent ginger tea brings me back to our room. I think I will do better staying attached to my form here than wandering off into realms beyond imagination.

I feel The Hooded One smile, and she starts telling a story about some obscure adventure of Zeus's time on Earth. I don't remember any of the details, but it kept me riveted in my chair until I finished several cups of tea.

***

I spend the next several days researching obscure versions of the stories. Orion, or a hunter in some form, appears in almost all of the ancient stories of the sisters. I find nothing that hints of the connection other than obsession. Maybe The Hooded One can enlighten me next time we meet.

114

***

I am sitting with a cup of pomegranate green tea wrapped by my hands to contain the warmth. It comforts my stiff fingers as the mellow fire in the background comforts my soul. Even more comforting is the hooded figure that sits opposite me in quiet company. How long have we been thus and I was not aware?

"I accompany you always in one energetic form or another, Little One. We have more of Orion's story to explore this night. What does obsession and insatiable passion have to do with the Seven Sisters? Perhaps the answer will be revealed as we go along."

Her arm is rising as she speaks. I take a deep breath to prepare myself and off I go into the light once more.

***

Artemis was hunting in the wild lands near Mount Taygeta, one of her most favorite places to hunt where game was plentiful and varied. The rugged terrain challenged even her skills. She had been following the tracks of a group of wild boar for about an hour when she felt the presence of Orion. Again! That boy was so befuddled and obsessed with the Seven Sisters. Usually, she or Taygeta laid an enchantment on the land so Orion just wandered around in circles. Artemis was feeling benevolent today so she flared her energy and called him to her. Perhaps he could join her in the hunt today, a partner to help with the tracking.

When Orion entered the small glen, he was excited and aroused from her calling. Artemis gave him one of her famous glares; she was a fierce warrior. Her hunting skills extended beyond killing animals and most men knew not to mess with her. Orion sat down on the nearest rock and quickly looked in another direction, causing Artemis to almost chuckle, since her dogs had the same reaction to her look. Maybe she could do something with the boy.

"Hail, Orion. How are you today? How's the hunting going?" Orion seemed a little shocked by her greeting, but he responded in kind.

"Hail Artemis, Great Protectress. I am well. My hunting forays in this forest are never fruitful."

Artemis warmed toward the boy with his obvious recognition of her status. She would bait him only a little today.

115

"Perhaps today is the day that your hunt will be fruitful. I could use a hunting companion."

The change in Orion's demeanor was instantaneous. He leapt up from the rock and swaggered towards her. "I would love to be your companion in the hunt."

Artemis stared at Orion thoughtfully. He needed a good run through the forest to use up some of his energy. "I am tracking a herd of wild boar. Can you track and run at the same time?" Orion seemed nonplussed. "Of course," he replied.

Artemis smiled at him. "Then let's go. The trail leads that way and they have a head start of about a half hour." Artemis picked up her gear and walked toward a small trail heading west. When Orion hesitated, she barked, "I expect my companions to take the lead on the hunt. The day is getting late. If we don't move quickly, the boar will be lost. Take the lead and move swiftly."

Orion nearly jumped out of his skin and squawked at her command. He moved forward after spending only a few minutes inspecting the trail. He flashed her a beautiful smile and then took off running through the dense underbrush. Artemis smiled as well as she took off after him. Hunting was her most favored activity. Well, almost her favorite. Then she had to focus on her footing.

Orion was moving swiftly in pursuit of the boar. Artemis was impressed with his tracking skills. Even she could not track and run any faster. As they ghosted through the forest, Artemis breathed in the fragrant air, the depth of smells from flora and fauna adding a rich array to the scent of the forest. They eventually came to a rocky area at the base of the mountain. Orion slowed down and then halted. He looked at her and shrugged.

“We are likely to lose the trail here."

Artemis nodded in agreement and started scanning the rocks above them. She knew they were close. She spotted the largest male sunning on a rock a good distance away. Her augmented vision was a gift of her goddess blood. She pointed silently and Orion followed her gaze. She could tell from his reaction that he could see the boar as well. She whispered, lest the sound of her voice echo up the mountain. "Orion, you have your father's eye."

Orion smirked as he whispered back, "Which one? I have three."

***

I am abruptly pulled back to the room with The Hooded One. I catch my breath and look at her. Why was I pulled out of that scene so suddenly? Her response astounds me. She is sending me off without a word. She raises her arm and points into the light. Off I go.

***

This time I am at a feast. Lots of food and drink. I recognize Zeus; the two gods sitting next to him seem familiar but I can't quite place them. Zeus is just finishing a story of one of his exploits and they are all laughing.

Zeus turns to the gentleman who is obviously the host. "Hyrineus, when are you going to get a son like my Hermes, here?" Zeus places his arm across the shoulders of the god sitting next to him. Ahh, Hermes is all grown up and quite handsome like his father. He has Maia's eyes. Then I realize that Hyrineus is Alcyone's son. We are in Boeticia. Why is The Hooded One bouncing me around Greece?

Hyrineus leans towards Zeus. They have all had a little too much to drink. "It's not like I haven't tried. Maybe I should petition you for a son. How many bulls do I need to sacrifice?"

The look on Hyrineus's face belies the lighthearted request he is making of Zeus. I see the look of a man begging for something he thinks he will never have. I can tell from Zeus's face that he sees it as well. I am not sure if it is Zeus or the alcohol that answers, maybe a little of both. Zeus leans in close to Hyrineus, but his voice is booming as he answers.

"Your strong wine and delicious food are boon enough for your request. I will make you a son tonight."

Hermes is looking thoughtful during the whole conversation. Poseidon is giving his son, Hyrineus, the look of a father who will grant his son anything. Hermes speaks up before Zeus can get up to find Hyrineus a woman. "Zeus, I have had an experiment in mind for a while. This might be the perfect time to try it."

Poseidon raises an eyebrow at Hermes's statement. "Is there something we haven't experimented with yet?" The laughter drowns

117

Hermes's response. It was several minutes and many raucous comments later before Hermes could continue presenting his idea.

Hermes pounds his beer stein on the table to get their attention again. "There is something we haven't experimented with yet. Sex magic without the female present. I think we can make a son for Hyrineus without using a woman for the mother."

The table got quiet. Hermes doesn't even squirm under the glare he got from his father, and carries on with his idea. "We need a place with strong feminine energy from the earth. There is a cave nearby that has been used for years for pagan fertility rituals. Hyrineus does need to kill an ox, a female one, and he must skin the hide himself and bring it to the cave in the dark of the moon. We will provide the creation energy to bring in a masculine soul to be birthed in the womb of the earth just like the birth from a mother." Hermes gestured grandly to the three men around him.

The silence of the table had turned thoughtful. Zeus took a long drink of his wine and as he set the mug down, he turned to Hermes. "Have you thought about how you would generate birthing energy in the ritual?"

Hermes shrugged as he replies, "I thought you and Poseidon have more than enough experience to come up with a plan."

***

Once again I am pulled from the scene. There isn't even a brief stop with The Hooded One this time. I am back with Artemis and Orion where they had left off. Artemis is smiling as she answers his question. She knows better than to praise only one of his fathers for a good hunting eye.

"You had three fathers and you only have two eyes. One of them gave you great sight." Orion smirked at her choice of words. He drew up his bow and arrow and the arrow flew through the air straight to the heart of the boar they could barely see. He brazenly bragged, "I got a lot more from my fathers than a good eye."

Artemis was very impressed with the shot. Even she might have missed that one. Her mood turned to dismay as Orion fired off four more arrows and killed off the entire herd. Orion turned to her with his face full of arrogant pride. He fully expected her to be so impressed with his hunting prowess that she would fall prey to his sexual charms. He was nonplussed to see the look of disapproval on her face. "What?" was all that came from his lips instead of his planned seductive rejoinder.

Artemis was furious and the fury in her voice shook the trees around them as she answered. "There is no need to hunt to excess."

Orion's face showed that he just didn't comprehend it. "I hunt whatever I please. I will hunt until there is nothing left to fall to my arrows and knife." The forest around them got quiet at his words. It seemed as if even the rocks had heard his words. Artemis knew this was the time of choosing, even if Orion was too thickheaded to feel the change. The lack of feminine energy in his birthing showed up as excessive and thoughtless pursuit. Perhaps she could guide him to better choices.

She relaxed her stance and slapped Orion on the back in a gesture of camaraderie. "Come. Let's clean up our kills. This is best discussed on a full stomach. I enjoy having a good comrade on the hunt." Orion brightened. Maybe he would get his chance yet.

***

The Weaver paused. Here was a knot in the weave that needed rethreaded. As she weaved the light of Artemis into the knotted thread of Orion, she shook her head. It remains to be seen if light to dark healed the pattern in this one.

Chapter Eleven

"The missing piece is the finished puzzle, Ignomatius. Let it be empty and place yourself within the puzzle as the last piece. Wholeness, completion, must hold that which is unknowable as part of the pattern."
The Hooded One

I am sitting across from The Hooded One. It has been a few days since my last journey, but we are just getting to the debriefing now.

"Debriefing? You have been watching too many spy movies, Ignomatius. Your journeys are a part of your spiritual path. I am your guide, not your handler."

You are more than a guide to me, dear Hooded One, but sometimes I feel like a spy as I watch the lives of the Seven Sisters unfold.

"When you can see through the story to the underlying patterns, you will hold the key to the spiritual quest that lies within your heart. Your journeys are for you, not the Seven Sisters."

Let's hope I don't wind up like Orion, arrogant and insatiable.

"As you saw, Orion was a unique experiment by the gods of Olympus, a failed experiment some would say. Balancing the masculine with the feminine is essential in the creation process; Orion was created through a process that was unbalanced, and it affected him deeply. We will revisit him again, but in the meantime, you have one more sister to meet: Sterope."

I was wondering if I was going to meet her.

"Meet her you will and her whole dysfunctional family." The Hooded One's arm starts to rise. There is a smile in her voice as she speaks again. *"I know how much you enjoy wild chariot rides. This story is full of them."*

Oh no! And off I go into the light once more.

I am glad The Hooded One gave me a small warning because I am indeed on a chariot racing at break neck speed. This time, at least, I am not plastered to the front. I seem to be riding in the back of a chariot with a powerful looking driver and an exceptional team of horses. Even Artemis would be hard put to control this team. We are racing through the streets with crowds of people watching. We fly past a grandstand and then he slows the chariot just a bit and waves to two radiantly beautiful women looking down upon the raceway. My heart leaps as I recognize the women: one is Sterope and the other is her daughter, Hippodamia. I realize that it must be Oenomaus driving the chariot.

Quickly he glances behind us. I turn to see another chariot racing two or three lengths away. Those horses seem to be laboring at this point. Small wonder, since legend had it that there were no horses in the land who could best Oenomaus's mares. He drove them as if his life depended on it, because as far as Oenomaus knew, it did. It had been prophesied that the suitor of his daughter, Hippodamia, would kill him. Oenomaus had declared that in order for a suitor to win Hippodamia's hand, he had to beat Oenomaus in a chariot race. Tricolonus, on the chariot behind us, was the thirteenth suitor to try. From the looks of the mares as they struggled to keep up, he would be the thirteenth one sacrificed because of the prophecy. Oenomaus reigned supreme. No one would have the hand of his lovely daughter.

With the weight of that thought, a wash of darkness seemed to pass over the chariot. I was suddenly thrown off the chariot and landed in what appeared to be a banquet hall. I wish I could say I landed tidily, but even the patrons noticed a rattling of the dishes as I lay upon the floor catching my breath. Thankfully, Artemis had stopped the chariot to let me off. I certainly hope this is my last ride here.

Oenomaus and Hippodamia are at the head table in the banquet hall. I hear talk of a new head posted above the gates today. How interesting that the voices sound proud of their king as he slaughtered suitor after suitor. What was more interesting was the behavior of Hippodamia at the head table. She was not a somber maiden who had just lost a potential love. Her face lit up as her father talked to her. The king leaned in a little too close and he gently stroked a lock of hair back into her luxurious tresses. Hippodamia melted in that soft feminine way that women do when a lover's touch pleases them. What am I seeing here? Surely I am misreading a cultural pattern from ancient times. I stand aghast, unseen amidst the merrymakers.

Then I see her: Sterope. There is no mistaking one of the Seven Sisters now. She is leaving the banquet room and walking to the balcony. As she gets to the doorway, she looks directly at me and does that slight nod of the head that invites one to join. I make my way through the crowd slowly, still stunned by the revelations of the moment. When I get to the balcony, Sterope is standing and staring out over the river, her stillness enveloping the whole area. For a moment, I think I am mistaken and it is a statue, not the goddess herself. Then she turns toward me and I am enveloped by a mixture of sadness and joy, I stumble and fall to my knees, speechless and lightheaded by the onslaught of her emotion.

Sterope walks over to me and lifts me up as she speaks. "I am so glad you have finally come, Ignomatius. It means that my sojourn on Earth is nearly done." She leads me to the railing and we both stare into the night. Her serenity supports me. Her sadness touches the very deepest parts of my soul that yearn for more. The bittersweet, existential conundrum of human existence is laid bare by her mere presence: love and joy mingled with deep betrayal and abandonment.

Sterope begins her story as if we had already been talking about it. "I do love Oenomaus. That was one of the true surprises of coming to the Earth Plane. Humanity captured our hearts. Then they betrayed our hearts, as they betray each other's hearts. We thought we would be above the effects of Form and on many levels, we are, but the heart is still vulnerable, for it is the connection to Source. Though I understand the ways of the heart, I am still ruled by it."

I interrupt her with questions that I have long awaited to have answered. How is the heart our connection to Source? What are the ways of the heart? Why does it rule us so? Can it ever be mended once it is broken?

Sterope turns towards me and gently caresses my face like a mother would in comforting her favorite child. I am so deeply touched. How is it that she touches me, unlike the other sisters?

Sterope reaches out and places her hand gently on mine as it rests upon the railing. "Ignomatius, you have become more real to us as you travel back and forth through time and space. You honor us by being our witness in ways you cannot even imagine. While your journey is to witness, your energy also becomes a catalyst, not unlike how one works in chemical reactions. Our experiences are affected by your presence and it affects how our energy shows up in future generations of humankind. So, yes, I can touch and comfort you now, but it is as much because you are receptive to it, as it is that I see how your presence stimulates changes in my reality."

"As far as your questions about the heart and love, your life journey will teach you the answers to these questions. Learning the true meaning of love is the journey we are all on. It is as simple and as complicated as that."

She grows still again. I experience the stillness of time as it must be at its core. I am still too agitated to remain in this state and I blurt out, "What happened with Oenomaus and Hippodamia?" I feel the disturbance within her, like a sharp wind blowing through us. Still her voice is soft as she answers.

"I taught Oenomaus some of the deepest mysteries. His mares are more than just good breeding; they are a combination of magic and light. Oenomaus was a masterful student, but the prophecy threw him off the path. An oracle said to beware of death from a son-in-law, which is how he and those around him chose to interpret it.

"There was no convincing him otherwise. It was disturbing to see him so obsessed. Then there was beautiful Hippodamia, who adored her father. His obsession with the prophesy darkened his mind and twisted his heart. He wanted happiness for our daughter, but he wanted to live. Hippodamia, whom he loved the most, would also be the vehicle of his death at the hand of her suitor.

"Somewhere in that tangled maze of love and betrayal, Oenomaus lost his way on his journey to the meaning of love. The dark paths of the heart led him to pervert his fatherly love. Hippodamia went with him without ever realizing the violation to her soul, as children follow their parents in their need for love."

Sterope goes into her stillness once again. My heart is in turmoil now as well. Surely the light of one of the Seven would have made a difference in the outcome. Sterope turns to me again.

"We truly did not understand the ways of the human heart, not even our own. The heart seeks love, that is a given and it must give love, that is understood. Humanity has confused love with hormonal responses and dark emotions. Jealousy is a pattern we could never experience until we took form. Jealousy is fear run rampant within the heart.

"There is the fear of not being enough for the ones we love. It twists and tangles the heart like mangled trees after a tornado. There is the libido, designed as a reminder of our connection to Source, which clouds the mind with unwise choices. All of this surrounds a heart that needs love. Humanity seeks love as they know it, whether it is the pure light of God or the dark paths of the heart. Hippodamia's next suitor comes from an equally dark path as her own. She will be drawn to his darkness like a moth to a flame. She only knows love as a forbidden darkness.

"Pelops was used by his father, Tantalus, in sex magic. Tantalus wanted the power of the gods. His heart was filled with lust for power. Tantalus used Pelops to try to gain that power in the ancient rites of Demeter. Pelops was nearly killed by the backlash of the energy when the working went awry.

"Poseidon saved him and carried him off, but even the sweet love of Poseidon would not heal Pelop's heart. He seeks love as he knows it and that will bring him here, where a father's love has betrayed the sacred trust of a parent to a child." Sterope's face is darkened as she tells the story and there are traces of tears on her cheeks. I bow my head to her sorrow and everything around me fades.

***

I am standing in a stable! One would think I would get used to moving from one tableau to a distinctly different setting, but my mind never seems to be prepared for the change. So, to a stable from a grand banquet and beautiful Sterope. I will try to avoid the horse manure, since I am sure The Hooded One would not appreciate me bringing it back with me.

If these are Oenomaus's mares, they are truly magnificent. I am not a horse person, but anyone could see the power and spirit of these animals. They all look at me as I think the word "animals". Oh, they are so much more, awake and aware and intelligent. I take a step back as their focus on me doesn't feel very friendly. They are stamping and snorting insults my way, I am sure. Someone comes to the stalls when they hear the ruckus from the mares. He is strong and swarthy but his voice is gentle as he soothes them. He turns my way and says, "It's about time you got here." I am startled. I don't know how to respond. Then I realize that he is looking beyond me. I turn and another man is standing behind me, watching the mares with avid eyes. Pelops! He is here. The stable man must be Oenomaus's charioteer, Myrtilus.

Their eyes are full of darkness as they size each other up. Myrtilus is the first to speak. "Come all the way in so no one sees you. The stables are quiet this time of night, so we can talk in private." Pelops walks over to one of the mare's stalls. There is envy in his voice as he says, "These horses are magnificent. Too bad that Oenomaus will not share his breeding tricks. There are few who could best them in a race."

Myrtilus nods. "I have seen your horses and they are of good stock, worthy of praise and I am sure they have won many races. They won't beat these girls here though."

Pelops turns to Myrtilus with his face veiled as he answers. "And I have seen the heads on the wall. I do not wish to have mine hanging there after tomorrow."

Myrtilus picks his words with care. "I have served Oenomaus for many years. He is not an easy man to serve. The mares keep me here. There are none like them and I would not have them in the hands of lesser grooms."

Pelops has a small smile on his face as he answers. "They could be yours for the asking."

Myrtilus snorts like one of the steeds in the stalls. "Not nearly a high enough reward for treason. Do not think this has not been offered before. I have access to the mares in all the ways that matter to me."

Pelops snaps back a little too quickly. "Half the kingdom if I win the race." Obviously, he has given this some thought.

Myrtilus shakes his head. "That, too, has been offered to me. You are not the first to try to subvert this old stableman. I have no need of kingdoms."

Pelops stands deeply in thought. Myrtilus fidgets. The longer they negotiate, the more likely they will be found out.

Pelops's voice is soft as he gives his next offer. "What if I offered you something more beautiful than these mares?"

Myrtilus looks at him in disbelief. "None are more beautiful than the horses that are before you now."

Pelops turns toward Myrtilus and the full force of his personality rings through his words. "I offer you the first night with Hippodamia."

Myrtilus is still for just a few seconds. Then a smile covers his face. "Now that is something that has not been offered before."

Pelops's voice as he answers carries the intensity of his desire to live. "It is being offered now. I want this kingdom and this woman. I am willing to pay any price to get it."

The gleam from Myrtilus's eyes mirror the gleam from the eyes of the mares in the stalls. Tension fills the stable as we all stand still waiting for an answer. "Deal!" Myrtilus nods and turns away.

"But how will you do it?" Pelops queries to his back.

Myrtilus turns with a very different gleam in his eyes to respond. "Leave it to me, youngster. Just make sure you keep your end of the bargain. I may only be a groom, but the blood of Hermes runs through me. I am not one to be thwarted."

Pelops stiffens, but his face is just as stony as Myrtilus's is ardent. "You will get your reward. That is my word."

I stand aghast as the two men walk away. Oenomaus's life hangs on the lust of two men, one with lust for power and one with lust for a woman. How many times throughout history will this pattern be repeated?

I know from the legends that the simple removal of a linchpin on the chariot fulfills the prophecy for Oenomaus. Pelops does not fulfill his part of the bargain and Myrtilus dies, as do the magic enhanced mares. I stand and stare at the mares. Oenomaus's secret will be lost and there will be nothing like these mares again for centuries. I feel a soft touch on my shoulder and turn in dismay. Sterope stands behind me.

"Their secret goes with me," she says softly. "They are a great example of what the union of human consciousness with animal consciousness can do, but the use of that union has been violated with the use it was put to. They are aware of the stakes of the race. The fear and distrust that created this whole drama spills into their consciousness. It sullies the spirit of Horse. Perhaps when humanity is ready I will return with this secret."

I don't know how to respond. There are so many emotions around me that I cannot sort out my thoughts. I could still feel the lust of Myrtilus and Pelops, the loyalty of the mares, Sterope's sorrow, and the forbidden passion of Oenomaus for Hippodamia. The darkness all around me could not be penetrated, even by Sterope's gentle presence. Why does God make us so? Surely this is some kind of cosmic mistake that makes the human heart the key to our enlightenment and the downfall of our race.

Sterope touches her finger to my lips. I must have been vocalizing my thoughts. We no longer stand in the stables but are on a gray plain outside of time and space. Sterope's radiance shines like a beacon here.

"As does your radiance, Ignomatius. I have brought you here to shield you from the energetic resonance of Oenomaus's palace. Your heart, at this moment, stands at a crossroad that faces all of humanity. The apparent betrayal of God versus his gift of life and love. How do you reconcile this?"

I have never met anyone who has reconciled it. Quite frankly, I don't know if it can be reconciled. God is not all that accessible on the Earth Plane. When the religious leaders say that the ways of God are inscrutable, they speak the truth.

"God is all around you and within you, Ignomatius. If you want access to God, study the intricate beauty of a flower or the connection of a mother to her child or the dance of flora and fauna as they feed upon each other in the flow of life."

It is not her words that reach me so much as the look of knowing that is in her eyes.

"God is so beyond the concepts of human consciousness. That which is the divine matrix of creation holds the pattern of life and guides it to completion. Just because you cannot see how your experience blends into the beauty of that creation does not mean that a divine consciousness does not exist or does not care. It is perhaps one of the more difficult limitations of being human, that ceiling of understanding. Know that humanity was created with love and grace. That grace flows through you, even as you stand on the brink of disaster or in the throes of betrayal."

So how do we find our way? How do we move on with our hearts broken into pieces from love scorned or betrayed? How does that serve God?

"You already have the answer. It is so simple and so difficult at the same time. This is the crux of the human experiment. Choose love over fear. Get back up and try again when life and love have knocked you down. Believe in the goodness of your own heart and the hearts of those around you. Forgive their mistakes and your mistakes as well. Forgive the perceived mistakes of God. They are lessons on the path to wholeness, not punishment. Beyond the veil is only light and love. Love is so misunderstood by humanity and yet it is the driving force, the reason for being."

Her voice is ringing through me and at the same time she is more distant as she speaks. She is fading away. I am adrift in my dreams, trying to fit together the pieces of the puzzle. Each attempt leaves something missing and I start again. New dream. Same pattern. I stand before another puzzle, with the final piece missing. Then I hear The Hooded One's voice.

"The missing piece is the finished puzzle, Ignomatius. Let it be empty and place yourself within the puzzle as the last piece. Wholeness, completion, must hold that which is unknowable as part of the pattern."

I step into the puzzle and even though I can see the puzzle isn't finished, I can see its integrity with or without all the pieces. Then I fall into the deep sleep that holds no memories of dreams. Only peace.

I awaken to the soft early morning sounds of spring. The birds are singing their joyous songs in the darkness just before the first morning light. The light cacophony of the birds is more comforting than annoying: the promise of a new day, of life renewing itself. The psychic silence of the world before humanity awakes.

Yet my heart aches. The news is full of the Hippodamias of the world: children who have lost their way, led by parents whose hearts seek love as desperately as their biological charges. The Pelopses of the world: those who lead the masses and seek to satiate their lust for power, destroying all who get in their way. The Oenomauses: people on a spiritual path who corrupt the meaning and intent because of some misinterpretation or lack of trust.

"But the Steropes are here, and the Hooded Ones, people like you, Ignomatius. The light is always there. Look for it even in the dark."

The Hooded One's quiet voice invades my thoughts with a needed interruption at the moment.

"Have your cup of tea and then take a long walk through your neighborhood, Ignomatius. Look for the love, it is there. If you see darkness, send light and love. It makes a difference, even if that difference is not reflected in your news. Love will ease the ache in your heart. Love heals the world in small ways and in big ways."

It's always an interesting day when The Hooded One is counseling me before I get out of bed. I feel her go quietly, like the stillness before dawn. The early morning light is peeking through my windows. Perhaps a strong cup of Indian Assam tea in the British tradition with lots of cream and sugar would be just the thing I need right now. Bittersweet seems to be the tone of my day.

***

I am sitting with The Hooded One in her cozy room again. How many times have I become aware in my dreams of this scene unfolding? It feels like home, a home where I am safe. A place where I can always get a good cup of tea.

"Ignomatius, if I had known that tea would lure you here, I would have tried it many years ago."

We both laugh. It's a good laugh. My banter about tea is a way to avoid the misery in my heart. The pain and suffering in the world is weighing me down. The Hooded One reaches out and lifts up my chin to look me in the eyes. I only see the blank hood that surrounds her face, but I am still comforted by the gesture.

"Little One, suffering is one of the many means ego uses to keep you bound to flesh instead of bound to spirit."

But there is so much pain in the world!

"And so much love and beauty. Ego chooses to stay focused on the pain. It chooses to suffer because of the pain. That suffering keeps you vested in ego. Ego was designed as a tool to function in Form. Spirit is the driving force, not ego. Yet ego is also designed to do everything it can to keep you safe while you are in form, even so far as to deny Spirit when it feels threatened. One method it uses is to elevate suffering to a spiritual practice. The truth is, you suffer because you are mad at God. It doesn't matter why. There are probably hundreds of times in your life when it seemed that God wasn't there or didn't seem to care. Ego capitalizes on that anger to reign supreme. Pain is a side effect of learning. Forgive God. Forgive yourself, and move on."

If love is so simple why is it so hard?

"Simple does not always mean easy. Think of love and tell me what it means."

A glib answer dies on my tongue as I think of all my relationships and the many ways I experience love in this world. The love of my parents, siblings, friends, and lovers. My love of life and nature and pets. Do I know the meaning of love?

"While the power of love is simple, the expression of love in form is rich and diverse as it reflects the divine matrix you call God or Goddess."

That doesn't answer why it is so hard to love.

"It's not that it's hard to love. It is how you've been taught to love that makes it hard. People mistake power or lust or fear for love. Parents teach their children what they learned was love, even if it means inflicting pain. It's not that parents want to hurt their children. Everyone does the best they can with what they have in the moment. If you don't have a clue how to love, it's hard to teach it to someone else."

So how do I learn what love really means? How do I heal my heart? How do I love and not get hurt?

*"Ignomatius, life is the journey to **be** love. You are always on the journey to learn what love means. It's not meant to be completely mastered in one lifetime. You will know when you are getting closer to the real meaning of love when there is joy in your heart.*

"There are three things you can do to heal your heart. The first is forgiveness. Forgive your parents. Forgive yourself. Forgive God. The second one is gratitude. Learn to give gratitude for whatever comes your way. See the gift in all of your experiences. Recognizing the gift will give you the lesson that comes with it. The third is to choose love over fear. In order to do that, you must recognize your fears and find the courage not to let them rule you. Choose to let love rule in your heart. The roots of love run much deeper than the roots of fear. Nurture love and love will nurture you.

"Lastly, Little One, I live in the Light. There is no pain there, only Light. You are bound to the illusion of Form. When you love, there will be great joy, and there will be pain as well. Ride the tumultuous waves of love with an open heart. This is the gift you bring back to God; that you have loved well. It will steer you home despite the challenges of Form."

And should I wrap that gift before I give it to God?

"Do not be cynical, Ignomatius. It does not become you or our work. There are many ways to deny your connection to Source. Cynicism is one of them."

I guess I need to think about this some more.

"Well, go and do that. When you are ready, we have another journey."

Where will this one be?

"We will talk about that when your mind and heart are clearer. Dream well, Little One."

***

My dreams are about being left behind by friends who drove off to the next adventure without me. As I lay there, feeling bereft and angry from the dregs of my dream, I remember a dream technique. I go back into the dream and my friends come back to find me. They didn't realize that I wasn't in the car. They couldn't and wouldn't travel without me. I feel better as I go about my day. Maybe the delicate flavor of Golden Monkey tea this morning with just a little bit of honey will help my mood. Then a hearty breakfast of tofu scramble and a long bike ride. Hopefully, the exercise will help my brain process all that resides in my heart.

"That and a couple of lifetimes."

I laugh at The Hooded One's joke and at the same time think that it is probably true. I am fine in this moment and that's the best I can hope for today.

Chapter Twelve

"Humanity is watched over and guided and deeply loved. Never doubt that. While the polarities of light and dark seem stark and glaring at this point, the balance point is only a thought away."   The Hooded One

I am back with The Hooded One, with a return to my jolly self and ready for another journey.

"And are you going a-pirating, jolly Ignomatius?"

Oh, is this journey going to be about pirates? I could use some treasure. Although, I don't remember any pirates associated with the Seven Sisters.

"The only treasure here is what is in your heart, which is worth a lot more than you think."

Well, the treasure in my heart doesn't pay the mortgage, but I will take your word that it is valuable.

"Are you ready for your next journey, Little One?"

I think so.

"Good. I think you will enjoy this one. We are going back to visit Electra one more time."

Electra! I hope she is not getting into trouble again.

"All will be revealed. Make sure you are well grounded before we start. The ritual you are about to witness is a powerful one and the effects are only coming to fruition in your present day."

So Electra gets it right this time?

"You'll see. Your old friends, Lycus and Chimaerus will be there as well. And Lycus's father, Poseidon."

I wouldn't exactly call Lycus a friend. Is this where I get eaten by werewolves?

"As far as I know, you never get eaten by werewolves. You have been ingested by a giant octopus. Was that so bad?"

Okay. I'm just going to sit here and do my "light and love" mantra. I am light and love. I am light and love. The Hooded One starts to raise her arm. Perhaps one of these days, I may actually be ready for what awaits me on the other side of the light.

***

I am so not ready for what I see this time. I am in a temple somewhere. And there are several people doing… um…having, um. Well, from the looks on their faces, they are having drug induced sex. It's sort of like walking into a Fellini movie set.

"They are initiates who have ingested kykeon, which does release the inhibitions of the mind, Ignomatius."

I turn to see who is speaking to me. Electra?! I am sure my mouth is hanging open.

"While this might have some interest to you, the real event that you are here to witness is through that door over there."

She points toward a large door across the room. The door is ornately carved, but I can't make out the details from here.

"Come with me."

I follow her across the temple space, looking very carefully at her back. It's no use. Several people are saying her name with such reverence. She just nods their way and keeps moving. At one point, someone grabs my leg and I scamper closer to Electra. I will have a word with The Hooded One when I see her again. Of course, she will tell me it's all light to her.

Electra turns to me and says, 'Do not make light of The Hooded One!" There seems to be a slight smile on her lips as she admonishes me. Is she making a joke? Thank goodness we are at the door. Then I realize that I don't know what is on the other side.

"Ignomatius, focus. We are about to enter the most sacred part of the ritual space. Do not profane it with your thoughts."

I am unnerved by the scene I just walked through. I take a deep breath and focus on The Hooded One and the cup of tea that awaits my return. I am sure it will be something calming like chamomile or lavender tea. I am still babbling.

Electra stops short of the door and turns toward me. She reaches out and touches my heart. "Focus here. Your spiritual connection is strong. Let Spirit rule you in this time and space. I wish to be finished with my work here so that I may return to the light. You are a catalyst. I need your energy to accomplish my work.

133

Don't let me down now just because you were not prepared to witness the Rites of Demeter."

Her touch grounds me and I feel her answering smile in my heart. There is a goodness all around us. I focus upon the intent rather than the act. I am ready. Electra waves her hands and speaks a few words and the door opens.

"Not everyone can pass through this door, Ignomatius. If you are not ready, you will not pass through."

Electra steps through the door. I briefly gaze at the strange and enigmatic runes that surround the door, close my eyes and step through. The smell of exotic spices is my first indication that I made it through. Then I smell the animal muskiness of Lycus, and the sweet innocence of Chimaerus. I open my eyes and find them staring at me.

Lycus growls and smiles at the same time. Chimaerus is pleased with himself, he is beaming. I am not sure that he really sees me. He has the look on his face of someone who is seeing an inner vision rather than the world around him. Perhaps he has partaken of the kykeon as well.

Inside the inner temple it is dark, as there are no windows. I see ornate carvings everywhere. I sense movement on the walls and columns but when I look at them directly, they are still. I feel a presence in one corner, darkness that my eyes can't adjust to. It moves and I realize it's another one of the gods: Poseidon! Even as I think his name, the temple becomes illuminated.

Electra, Lycus, and Chimaerus are standing in the center. Electra has her right hand raised with the right hands of Lycus and Chimaerus on either side of her hand. They are standing so close together, the power in the room is dizzying.

Poseidon's deep voice fills the room as he starts a chant to call in the Seen and Unseen powers to protect the sanctity of the work. The three in the middle stand as if they are transfixed, living statues of light with their power swirling around them.

***

Electra has been working for this moment since the last attempt at Olympus failed. She smiled briefly to herself. Not so much a failure as it was a learning experience. Her glimpse of the time lines before she crashed taught her a lot about how the Weaver worked the lines.

She had enlisted her sisters' help this time, as well. Celaeno had genetically engineered her sons for this work. The Light and the Dark were in perfect balance between Lycus and Chimaerus. Merope and Sisyphus had been focusing their energy work toward this change. Sisyphus had been ghosting in and out of the temple space to anchor their energy for today. Maia was the grounding point as she sat in deep meditation in her cave. Taygeta had worked with the patterns of the lines to help focus the energy. Sterope held the life force energy patterns, while Alcyone connected with the stars. The one thing Electra had learned was the power of working in unity with her sisters rather than trying to create change by herself.

***

As I watch Electra join her energy to Lycus and Chimaerus with the breathing exercises of the sex magic, I become aware of lines of energy coming from all directions. It feels as if each sister is physically present. As I feel their presence, six columns of light appeared in a circle around Electra, Lycus, and Chimaerus. Dazzling, dancing, pure Light. This was probably as close as I would get to experience the meaning of being in the Light.

***

It had taken Electra many years to understand the path of the Darkness that she had witnessed in her vision on the beach. Her initial reaction to stop the Darkness had nearly annihilated her and Zeus. She now knew that the Darkness was part of the Plan. On the physical plane, Light and Dark needed to find their balance, instead of the Light having to win over the Dark.

Electra held that thought of balance foremost in her mind as the energies in the room quadrupled with the arrival of her sisters in their light bodies. Her breathing pattern was in perfect sync with Lycus and Chimaerus as their bodies comingled in physical ecstasy. As she channeled the energy, she stepped into the place within

135

herself that could see and touch the timelines. The room and all the participants melted away from her perception.

***

Electra was swirling in a giant vortex of energy. It took her several minutes to get oriented to her vision. What was a minute anyway? She swirled in time after that thought. Balance! She was seeking balance! The swirling energy around her became the light and dark of Chimaerus and Lycus. She felt the touch of light, then the touch of dark. She was caught up in a humongous whirlpool of energy. The polarities of energy pushed her into smaller and smaller circles.

Balance! Balance in the timelines! She focused on the carefully laid out patterns she had crafted with Taygeta. She swirled deeper into the whirlpool, sinking rapidly toward the point of singularity that was the origin. Light and then Dark. Light and then Dark. She could no longer tell if she was swirling or if the lines swirled around her.

Suddenly, all sense of motion ceased. She was at the point of origin; the moment she had prepared for was at hand. Her foremost and only thought was "Balance!" The lines seemed to stand still here. The stillness was overwhelmingly thunderous in its quiet. She could see patches of light and darkness within the lines. She held the thought of balance and called upon the energy of the people who surrounded her body in the ritual. Balance! The hue of the light shifted subtly. She began to rise rapidly, but even at breakneck speed, she could see that the lines now alternated light and dark in equal balance. It would be interesting to see what had become of Lycus and Chimaerus after this working. That thought brought her fully back into her form which was taking deep, gulping breaths. She saw faces swirling around her and then she passed out.

***

Lycus and Chimaerus are gently holding Electra after she faints. It only takes a few minutes for Electra to become conscious again and she immediately hugs both Lycus and Chimaerus. I don't think I can describe what I had just witnessed. What my physical senses register does not match what happened energetically in the

136

room. I don't even know what an implosion would feel like, but this feels like one. Lycus is glowing rather than glowering. For the first time, I sense a groundedness in Chimaerus. He is no longer a boy on the verge of manhood. He stands proudly before the sisters. Wait. All the sisters are here in form at the same time. Now I feel like I might pass out.

It is a joyous moment for all. I am sure my mouth is hanging open as I watch them hug each other and celebrate the working. Sweet wonder fills the room. Poseidon is quiet in the corner but he glows just as much as the Sisters.

Lycus and Chimaerus go to Poseidon and he claps them on the back. Chimaerus winces a bit and then stands tall. Lycus crushes him in an embrace.

Food appears and everyone starts eating and chattering. It all seems so normal after such a momentous event. I remain the quiet observer of a history that has never been told.

Lycus leaves the crowd and heads directly toward me. As he approaches, he is turning into the wolf. If I had hackles, they would be up. He stops in front of me and I am struck by the look on his face as his wolf persona fades. Such innocence is there. I am almost taken in. He is trying to get my DNA for Celaeno again! He laughs as he changes his form. "Just thought I would try to give Mother a gift before Father takes Chimaerus and me to the Elysium Fields, our reward for doing such good work. We are no longer able to stay among humanity because our energy shifted into higher frequency patterns that might melt humans. Are you melting, Ignomatius?"

My form is not here so I think I am safe for the moment. The Elysium Fields? I don't think I have heard of them.

"One of the Mysteries. Most people would think of them as heaven, a paradise that transcends earthly energy. I'll send you a postcard."

Enjoy. You have earned your reward. It was magnificent to have witnessed your transformation. Lycus looks at me deeply to see if I am being sincere, which I am.

Chimaerus scampers over. "Come on, Lycus. Your father is ready for us." The young men walk over to Poseidon who takes their hands in his, and they all vanish into a bright light. At that point, all seven sisters turn to look at me. I nod my head in acknowledgement. Then I disappear into the Light as well.

***

The Weaver feels the surge of light come through the Weave after Electra's ritual. She watches Electra's knot unravel and move toward wholeness. She is always pleased when a knot unravels itself. She looks at Zeus's knot and it remains the same. Some threads come in knotted and go out knotted. She takes a look at the tangle of threads that represent Orion. Some knots just simply need to be redone. With a deep sigh, the Weaver starts pulling threads out of Orion's knot.

***

Did I dream after I left the Sisters? Did I sleep deeply? I must have slept. Waking up in my room is a wonder to me. I jolt awake and quickly look around, all by myself. Flashes of last night's journey are going through my mind, sort of like remembering a movie. Except for the joy in my heart, a joy beyond words. There is hope for the world and I know it in my heart. There must be a tea to match my mood this morning but I can't think of what it might be. Maybe I'll try them all, or settle for one of my favorites. There is nothing in my kitchen that can match the joy in my heart. I brew a white tea from China. As I sip the tea and watch the birds flitting around in the morning light out in my back yard, I remember being in the presence of all Seven Sisters at once. Some little bit of spiritual yearning in my heart has been satisfied. No. Make that a big yearning has been fulfilled. Being in their presence was as close to being with God as I may ever get. It was a transcendental moment. I have no idea how long I sat there, lost in thought.

***

I am sitting with The Hooded One once again. She's done some redecorating in our room. It feels brighter, yet still homey. My chair is a deep blue easy chair. The tea table is blue glass with beveled edges. It reflects the image of The Hooded One without revealing anything about her in the slightest way.

"It is your brain that has decorated this room, Little One. The changes wrought by the ritual are marked upon your soul and are reflected here."

You still seem the same, dear Hooded One.

"I exist outside of time and space, so I am not affected by happenings within time and space."

What does it look like outside of time and space? Do you have a home? A family? A spiritual bed and breakfast where you serve tea and wisdom?

"You have no words for my existence, that dimension is beyond the construct of words. This meeting space is as close to any manifestation of home that I would claim."

The Hooded One stops for a moment as if she has stumbled upon something she has never seen before. If this is home, then I am your family and you have all the love in my heart.

The Hooded One wavers and then shimmers like a hologram that is malfunctioning. Have I said something wrong? Am I going to lose her? I reach to touch her hand and she steps back and fades away. Oh, I have done something upsetting. I sit stunned in my chair. The fireplace crackles and my tea is cold. My heart feels like it is going to stop beating.

I wake up in my bed, alone with an emptiness deep inside. What have I done? There is no gentle voice answering in my head. I look at the clock and it is 3 am. I won't be getting any more sleep tonight, so I get up and start going through some Qigong exercises. Tears are streaming down my face. What have I done?

Time goes by. I exist. I work. I eat. The memory of The Hooded One is like a toothache, constant and sharp. I go to bed each night and hope to wake up in our room, only to be disappointed in the morning. Was it all a dream?

Then one night, I become aware that I am in the room once more. It is back to its humble décor and The Hooded One sits opposite me, my dear Hooded One.

"My dear Ignomatius, I am sorry that I worried you."

It was much more than being worried, but all is well now. What happened?

"I realized when I called this space home that it did indeed feel like home. You do indeed feel like family. I am attached to you and our journey. Not something I had anticipated as part of this experiment."

I am a bit offended. So am I like a guinea pig to you? The Hooded One leans in close and takes my hand.

"You are an amazing spiritual being. One that holds my attention. Don't belittle that."

I am somewhat mollified. Actually, I am ecstatic. Finally, we can talk about my last journey. I have been doing some research. There was a tomb built for Lycus and Chimaerus saying they died to end some great plague, but their bodies were not in the tomb because Poseidon had taken them to the Isles of the Blessed as a reward.

"I am surprised. That's a fairly accurate description, as human descriptions go, of great energetic events."

Well, do I ever get to visit the Isles of the Blessed?

"The mysteries surrounding the Isles of the Blessed and Elysium are a veil for an interdimensional shift. They are in another dimension, and once one goes there, there is no coming back to Form as you know it."

So I don't have to worry anymore about Lycus eating me?

"Not in this life, no."

Wait! It happens in some other life then? I feel the smile behind the hood. I think The Hooded One was just making a joke. Life has changed.

"But you do still have journeys before you, Little One."

I am not quite done with the last one. The sisters acted like their ritual was a great success, but if you look at the world I live in, light and darkness are not well balanced, nor have they been for the last several hundred years.

"Humanity has been on the spiral downward to the point of origin. Their journey reflects Electra's journey. There are those within humanity who are holding the focus of balance. There are Beings of Light who are holding the energy for the journey to be successful. Humanity is watched over and guided and deeply loved. Never doubt that. While the polarities of light and dark seem stark and glaring at this point, the balance point is only a thought away."

Then what can I do to help?

"That's a question that each person must ask themselves. The answer lies in the same realm as the question 'How do I love?' Seek balance. Just so you know, balance is not necessarily symmetrical, nor is living at extremes a healthy way to find balance."

What is the next step for us, dear Hooded One? The sisters have done their ritual. I have met them all. I had the honor of being with them collectively. Is that it?

"I am glad you asked. It is time to go visit our old friend, Zeus."

Zeus? Why Zeus?

"The story is not yet finished."

The Hooded One raises her arm and I go off into the light once more.

***

Zeus was in a rage. He was stomping around the same mountain where he had talked with Apollo and Orion. This time the avalanches were destroying the villages at the foot of the mountain. Lightning and thunder raged around Zeus. He crashed his hands together and a large boulder in front of him split in half. He twisted his hands and the pieces crumbled until the boulder was annihilated. Then he stomped some more, the mountain trembling beneath him. The results of his behavior were quite satisfying.

A shield of light created a calm space in the pouring rain and suddenly Poseidon was standing next to Zeus. Zeus growled at his visitor and called down a bolt of lightning on Poseidon. Poseidon remained unfazed. "Zeus, my brother, we have been down this road before. Calm yourself before you do something rash again and we both suffer for it."

Poseidon's calm demeanor seemed to have no effect upon Zeus, but the next bolt of lightning struck another boulder instead of Poseidon. "Why did the Pleiadians use you for their ritual and not me?" Zeus thundered above the storm. "I have been working with their magic for years. We share children. I am the most powerful!" Zeus's body literally puffed up as he shouted at Poseidon.

"Perhaps they needed more than just power for their ritual." Poseidon's quiet answer infuriated Zeus even more, but Poseidon remained calm. "Zeus, you betrayed their trust when you stole their power during sex magic. There are consequences."

Lightning bolts shot out of Zeus's eyes and landed at Poseidon's feet. Zeus raged. "Consequences?! I'll show them consequences. Where is Sisyphus? That worm will suffer the consequences for ratting me out for all eternity!" Zeus disappeared in a ball of flame and thunder.

Poseidon stood quietly and soaked up the rain and as it flowed off his form, the damage to the mountain was healed. As the turbulence disappeared, the storm became a gentle rain rather than a tempest. Poseidon turned towards me. "There are always consequences for misuse of power, Ignomatius. Even for us." With that Poseidon faded away and I was whisked off to another place and time.

***

I arrived just in time to see Zeus pop into Merope's and Sisyphus's castle. Merope was startled and then started to raise her hand in a gesture of power. Zeus was too quick for her. He grabbed Sisyphus and said, "You are not getting away this time, Sisyphus. You will suffer for all eternity!" Then they both disappeared. Merope slowly lowered her hand as she whispered, "Do not worry, my love. This was foreseen. All eternity is not that long."

***

Again, I am whisked away and this time I stand at the bottom of a long hill. Sisyphus is pushing a huge rock up the hill. The sinews on his arms and neck stand out as he strains to keep the rock moving. Sweat is rolling off of him. The boulder inches up the hill, looking like it will roll backwards at any moment and crush Sisyphus. Merope appears next to him, and a light shines through the dark shadows that surround Sisyphus. Merope speaks and her quiet voice is magnified in the chaos of Hades that surrounds us.

"Sisyphus, know that I cannot touch you as you labor for all eternity, but you will hear my voice and see my face each and every moment of the time you spend here. Eternity will pass. I will be waiting for you at its end. Your time will seem like but a moment. I have spoken. So let it be!"

Merope is gone and Sisyphus is still struggling to get the rock up the hill, but his eyes shine with the light of love. I stay to watch him make it to the top and see both him and the boulder appear again at the bottom of the hill. He pushes mightily and the rock inches up the hill. He does not suffer.

***

I am back with The Hooded One. A cup of tea awaits me. I sort of liked the blue glass tea table. Maybe I will redecorate a little bit. I can feel The Hooded One staring at me.

"I just love the way the human mind works. I've just teleported you all over ancient Greece and you come back and think about redecorating our room. Are our journeys becoming mundane to you, Ignomatius?"

Oh, no. Not at all. I love our journeys. The table is fine. I mean, I won't mess with anything ever again. I don't want to upset you like last time.

"Relax, Little One. The fact that you can surprise me is a good thing."

Zeus surprised me. His temper is known throughout history, but this time he was off the charts. I am surprised that Poseidon stayed so calm.

"Zeus and Poseidon have a long history together as brothers. At one point, Zeus, in his anger, chained Poseidon to a rock for all eternity. Poseidon wears it as a ring now. I think Zeus can remember that his temper gets out of control. Poseidon is the one who helped humanity, time and again. There was a reason he was the one at the ritual with the Seven Sisters and not Zeus. Poseidon can get just as angry as Zeus, but he is much more of a healer in his own way."

Will Sisyphus eventually wear that rock on his finger?

"That remains to be seen. Are you ready for one more journey tonight?"

Wow! We take a little break and you are all gung ho to move along.

The Hooded One starts to raise her arm. *"Gung ho, Little One? I don't think I have ever, in any dimension, been called gung ho."*

I sheepishly go into the light.

***

Orion is hunting. Well, it's more like stalking. Merope doesn't have Sisyphus around and Orion is hoping that now is his chance. So far, he has not managed to bed even one of the Pleiadians. His hunger for their energy has never abated; it is even

143

stronger than his desire to hunt, even though more hunting never sated his thirst to hunt. Perhaps today his thirst will be sated.

Merope is aware of Orion as he skulks around her castle. She is more than annoyed. It is hard enough to maintain her balance without Sisyphus with her. For a moment she considers dropping Orion into the nearest volcano, although that certainly wouldn't cool him down at all. Instead she sends a thought to Artemis. Let her deal with Orion. She seemed to like him and they certainly spent enough time together hunting.

Artemis appears close to where Orion lay hidden behind a tree as he stares at Merope's castle. She gives a deep sigh and the sound brings Orion to his feet with his bow and arrow pointed right at her. She arches her eyebrow and says, "Let me assure you there is nothing to hunt in that particular castle." Orion leers as he answers. "Not all creatures that I hunt end with an arrow through their heart."

Artemis grimaces at Orion's poorly veiled lust. "Orion, let it go. You are not going to bed any of the Seven Sisters or me, for that matter." Orion actually pouts. Artemis has a hard time not rolling her eyes in exasperation. As with all immature males, distraction was the easiest path. "I have found a great place to hunt boar."

Orion isn't as easily distracted this time. "I am on a hunt and you are not invited. Be gone with you." He says it with power and Artemis fleetingly feels the urge to leave. However, she was Artemis, Queen of All Beasts and the beast in front of her was being irritating. She steps in closer to Orion with her eyes ablaze at his insolence.

His eyes get wide as he realizes his mistake. No one challenges Artemis and lives. He backpedals quickly. "All right. All right. We will go hunting at your 'great' place." He couldn't keep the sarcasm out of his voice. He will not lose sight of his prey, so he pushes just a little harder even though he knows his life hangs in the balance. "But don't think any amount of hunting will slake my thirst. I will hunt and kill until all the animals are gone. None will escape me."

A chill runs through Artemis as he speaks the words, for she hears the truth of them. Orion is beyond help. At the same time, she feels the earth and forest around them get deadly quiet. Orion seems unaware of the heart beat that filled the silence. It is the heartbeat of

Gaia, spirit of the Earth itself. Something deadly is on its way because Gaia knows the truth of Orion's words as well.

"It is best if we get moving, Orion." Artemis calls up her chariot. As they disappear out of the glen, a scorpion appears on the grassy area where Orion had stood a moment before. It starts to follow the trail of the chariot. Orion will not survive its sting.

***

The scorpion has been chasing Orion for days. It had gotten much larger. He tried to kill it several times but no arrow would penetrate it, fire would not burn it, and it could not be crushed, even by big boulders.

Orion watched from his hiding place as the scorpion followed the false trail he had so carefully created. The cursed thing seemed to be telepathic as well, for as he watched, it stopped and looked his way, then started climbing directly toward his hiding place. He needed help and he could only think of one god powerful enough to help him slay the scorpion. The fact that he would need help slaying anything just got the bile churning in his stomach. He didn't have time to contemplate his dilemma, the scorpion was almost upon him.

***

Zeus was a bit surprised to have Orion pop out of nowhere. Zeus is still in a bad mood and Orion sets him on edge most of the time. Before he can even muster a querulous growl, the giant scorpion appears several yards away. Zeus looks at the haunted face of Orion and the slow approach of the scorpion. He recognizes the energetic signature of Gaia on what is now as big as an ox; even Zeus knows better than to mess with Gaia. Zeus grabs Orion and spirits him off to his cave where the wards inside will protect them for a while.

"What have you done, Boy? What set Gaia against you?" Zeus had Orion by the shoulders. He thinks he was showing amazing restraint by not literally shaking Orion like he was a child.

145

"Gaia? Is that who sent the scorpion? Where can I find her?" it was a measure of Orion's need that he doesn't react to Zeus calling him a boy.

"She's all around us and a part of us as well. One does not find Gaia, but sure as Hades, she has found you. What happened?" Zeus peers into Orion's eyes as if the answer can be found there.

Orin takes a step back and adjusts his chiton. "Nothing happened. I've just been hunting like I always hunt and this scorpion started showing up everywhere. I knew it was after me."

Zeus steps in closer to Orion. "How are you hunting?"

Orion smirks. "I hunt and kill everything in my path. I will hunt until there is nothing left to hunt. I hunt…"

Zeus claps his hand over Orion's mouth. The electric tingle down his spine as Orion was speaking gives him all the answer he needs. Orion has gone beyond the acceptable boundaries of being on Earth. It is time to send him home. In the meantime, he does not want the scorpion showing up at his cave. "Come! I have an alternate dimensional space set up where you will be safe until I can figure out what to do." Zeus gestures and the two disappear from the cave.

***

Zeus calls in Poseidon and Apollo to help with Orion. Orion doesn't like the serious looks on the faces around him after Zeus explains the situation. He likes it even less when Apollo puts his hand on Orion's shoulder and says, "I am sorry, Son. It's time for you to go."

Orion shrugs the hand off his shoulder. "Go where? What do you mean by that?

Poseidon answers, "Back to the light, Orion."

Chapter Thirteen

I am back with The Hooded One. Even though I know the endings of these stories, I am not prepared for the emotional onslaught I am experiencing. The Hooded One is speaking but I am not hearing her. I am seeing Orion's face when they told him he was going back to the Light; it was a mixture of righteous anger and rapturous joy.

Meanwhile, The Hooded One has noticed my inattention and stopped speaking. So how did the story end? Did the scorpion bite him or did Artemis shoot him with an arrow as some stories say? The Hooded One is quiet for a moment.

"Does it truly matter so much to you, Ignomatius? Orion was a good experiment with a bad ending!"

But did he die by the bite of retribution or by the hand of a friend?

"I see now what is bothering you. Pick the ending that you like the best. Either way, Orion was sent up into the heavens. The Seven Sisters are about to go now."

What does that mean, sent into the heavens?

"There are levels of what you call spirit. Remember that even as I say this, it is all illusion, because All is One. Your soul connects to your higher self, connects to spirit, connects to entity, and connects to greater Entity. Most people would consider greater Entity to be God or whatever their version of God means to them.

"Some greater Entities are embodied as stars in the physical realm. Not all stars contain evolving consciousness. Gaia is the spirit of the earth. Vesta Helios is the spirit of your sun.

"The Pleiades Constellation holds the greater consciousness of the Seven Sisters as you have come to know them. The human form does not yet have the ability to connect on that level. It is evolving toward the day when consciousness of Entity-self is as common as consciousness of who you think you are, as self.

"Orion's return to the heavens is not quite why you are here; his story is more of a side note. The Seven Sisters have called you to witness their lives, and they call you to witness their departure as well."

I am not ready to say goodbye. By departure, do you mean death? Isn't that what we are talking about here?

"Ascendancy is a form of death from the physical plane perspective. All beings and things return to the light. It is a return to what they truly are. Some beings evolve to a level of vibration that their return is more than a return; it is an evolutionary step up for humanity as a whole. Jesus is an example, or Mohammad or the Buddha."

So are you saying that the Pleiades are like Jesus?

"While they had a different purpose than Jesus, their effect has been just as lasting. Look to the legacy of their children: they came to affect the planetary evolution and humanity's as well. When humankind developed mass consciousness, it changed the course of this planet. Mass consciousness is developing as a tool to work with Gaia and the evolution of the Earth. The Seven Sisters all had effects on mass consciousness that targeted areas that would ultimately accelerate change in humanity and then allow a greater connection to their Entity."

You keep mentioning Entity like it is the highest authority on the spiritual chain. Are you saying there is no god?

"God, as most of humanity uses it, is a limiting term with many negative associations, such as the righteous, wrathful father in heaven. Source, which gives birth to All That Is, is beyond human concept. 'God' holds a small part of what Source means. All That Is, quite literally, means that everything you are and everything around you is part of Source expressed through All That Is, through Greater Entity, and down through entity. Again, All is One, but so much more than the human mind can conceptualize while it is in Form. Words cannot convey the essence of Source. Look at the incredibly rich expression of All That Is in form and you have a better understanding of Source."

So does God exist?

"There are gods and goddesses. There is God. There is Goddess. There is more beyond. Reach for the light to explore the beyond."

Well, God or Goddess, or Source, I am still not ready to say goodbye to the Sisters. I look at The Hooded One and my heart drops. She is raising her arm. Her voice is gentle as she speaks. *"But they are ready for you, Little One."*

And off I go into the light.

***

I arrive into a small grove of trees and see the Seven Sisters standing a short distance away. They are standing in small clusters, talking to each other. Zeus is there, Poseidon and Prometheus as well. The men are standing off to the side. They are all at the base of something huge. I step out of the grove to take a closer look. I look up and up and up. It is a tree with the most incredible array of branches I have ever seen. I am lost in wonder.

Sterope's voice pulls me out of my reverie. "Come, Ignomatius. The Tree of Life has been studied since the beginning of time by earthly mystics. You could stand there for lifetimes and still be mesmerized." She leads me by the hand over to her sisters. They turn and smile at us.

"It is time!"

I am not sure who speaks or if it is the collective voice of the Sisters. I am in awe to be in the presence of the Sisters all at the same time. So much beauty. So much power. It dwarfs the impression of the Tree of Life. Even Zeus is subdued in their presence.

Maia steps forward and all are quiet as she begins to speak. "My sisters, my friends..." she pauses to include the men in her gaze. Zeus actually blushes. Then her eyes turn toward me. I am lost in her eyes as she speaks again. "It is time for us to return to our light bodies. Our sojourn on the earth has given gifts beyond words to each and every one of us. The beauty of Gaia, as she has manifested in Form, has been more than worth our time here."

I look around at the sisters as Maia is speaking, and they are all glowing. A light shines from within them that is so holy. It is the only way I can describe it. As I watch, they are gathering into a shape like a six pointed star with Maia in the middle. Their light strengthens.

***

Suddenly, I am thrust away from the sisters and I feel like I am in two places at once. I am standing next to a sea and in the distance someone is swimming for their life. Orion! On the shore, Apollo is standing next to Artemis. Her arrow is cocked in her bow and she is watching Orion's head bob in the waves. Apollo is urging her to shoot now while Orion is close at hand. Artemis is shaking her head. She will give Orion a fighting chance to escape. I am in the waters with Orion. I see his body working in perfect rhythm to swim beyond the range of Artemis's arrow, but his mind is elsewhere. I follow the path of his mind….

And I am back in the grove watching the Seven Sisters. Orion's form is transparent as he watches them from his hiding point; he looks at me and smirks. "I never lose my prey. I will track them into the heavens if need be." I realize he has created a doppelganger and is in two places at once.

I leave the grove again, a bit shaken from my experience, only to be filled with bliss from the light of the sisters as they ready themselves to ascend. I was right. I am not ready for this experience at all. Too much, too fast.

One of the sisters comes to stand next to me and I immediately feel grounded. It is Taygeta. She speaks to me like the friend she is, even as she stands exalted in the light.

"The Tree of Life is a being of mathematical perfection, in perfect balance between that which is Above and that which is Below. It will look to you like we are traveling a path of light straight up the Tree, but there are steps and levels. We have already mastered the levels. Do you comprehend this so far, Ignomatius?"

I nod. I am emotionally overwhelmed at the moment but the clear, cool energy of Taygeta's mathematical mind is a welcome relief.

"What I am about to explain to you is the path out of Spirit into Form and from Form back to Spirit. The Tree works in both directions, just as a real tree does here. The roots are just as important as the branches and leaves or the trunk. They all have their function, and all are needed for the wholeness of the Tree. Make note that you came in from Spirit. You have already mastered Spirit to be in Form, think about that when you have time. It is a huge revelation for most of humanity."

But what about…

"We don't have time for questions, Ignomatius. Listen closely and you will absorb this on many levels. Understanding can come later and the knowing will open doors within your psyche.

"We are gathered in a six-pointed star because that is the symbol that represents the first level of power of the Tree of Life, or the last, depending upon your point of view. The six-pointed star symbolizes 'as above, so below.' This is the Physical Foundation, which is a balance of elements. It is wholeness; the coming together of both the physical and the spiritual.

"You will see Maia's energy in the center, move into a spiral. This is the symbol of the second level, which is Grace/Freedom. The spiral symbolizes that which opens doors without closing them. Grace is your connection with Spirit that keeps the flow going. It moves in the flow of the path that you are choosing to follow. It is the first part of your spiritual awakening. It puts you on your path, and allows you to function on that path."

As Taygeta speaks, I can see the symbol forming on the tree. A new symbol appears when she stops speaking. It is the infinity loop. As soon as Taygeta realizes that I have seen the third symbol, she continues on.

"The infinity loop represents the level called Victory which is related to creativity and the Higher/Group Mind. Everything is related to everything. It is never ending and a reminder that it is built on very much more than meets the eye. The process, itself, doesn't end. You are simply seeing a different piece of it at any given time. The victory in this process lies not so much in the actual success, but in the recognition of the path you may take there. Victory is not accomplishing, it is choosing to try."

Suddenly, the energy of the Seven Sisters turns into the colors of the rainbow. Taygeta pauses as I stare in wonder at the beauty before me.

"We are preparing your energy to travel the path of the Tree of Life, even as we prepare our own, Little One. It is not your time yet, but when you are ready to leave the Wheel, your path will be open to you.

"The rainbow is the symbol of the next step and it is called Beauty or Perfected Mind. The rainbow has all the colors of the spectrum, including the ones you do not see. Every piece of refracted light holds all the pieces of the rainbow, even though it is only a part of the whole. This is what you are, a part of the whole, and therein lies the beauty.

"The next step is called Strength and it is represented by a transparent cube. Strength is the ability to see beyond the surface to what is within. Strength is being able to love when the world around you is saying no."

I stop and take a breath. I feel like I am climbing the Tree and the world lies below me. Merope comes over and takes my hand and Taygeta's hand. She looks me deep in the eyes as she speaks.

"Ignomatius, you must stay grounded for this. You are here to witness but not to follow. Allow Taygeta to finish her description of our path. See it enough that you get the knowing, but don't lose your focus on your humanity."

I nod to Merope in understanding. The sisters have moved into a five-pointed star with Merope and Taygeta by my side.

Taygeta continues. "Mercy is the next level and it is represented by the five-pointed star. Mercy is the ability to move out of yourself, which gives birth to understanding. Mercy is the first level in the world with access to All That Is. All That Is' first act in the world is mercy to humanity. It has been transformed in the world where care and non-judgmental acceptance is needed."

At this point, Alcyone comes over and takes my hand as Taygeta rejoins her sisters. I am surprised by the gentleness in her voice as she speaks. "Ignomatius, I thank you for our journey together. Your courage to face my manifestations on all levels showed me a part of humanity I had never acknowledged."

I gaze at her eyes and see the stars dancing there. Alcyone remains a mystery to me. So little of her is in human form. She looks up the Tree and I follow her line of sight. Above the pointed star is a pyramid. Alcyone continues when she sees that I have seen the next step. "The next level, represented by a pyramid, is Forces of Transmutation. The pyramid holds the perspective of all sides of the triangle.

"Transmutation is change. It means becoming something 'other' than what we are. Creating something new requires a change from the old; it does not mean a loss of the old, it means a transformation of the old. Perspective creates the nature of transformation. Transmutation is the rope that ties you, not the struggle to free yourself from it. It is the part of you that is willing to be tied (spirit in physical form) in order to later become stronger."

Alcyone pauses and looks up again. Above the pyramid on the tree, two symbols appear side by side on the next level: a triangle and an equal armed cross. A Mona Lisa smile crosses her face as I look askance at her.

"The next step has two symbols: they are at the same level because the one needs the other in order to be complete. The equal-armed cross represents Wisdom and is the symbol of Spirit working in the world. Wisdom is the masculine aspect of Source. It is God energy. Wisdom is knowledge which has been gained from experience; it is love in action. It is the highest level of what knowing can access. God energy is the manifesting/active aspect of Source.

"The triangle represents Understanding: Form, Spirit, and Source. Understanding is the feminine aspect of Source. It is Goddess energy. Understanding is the 'seed' of your intent before it has flowered. It is the triunity of Source: you--the Source that you are as you know it--the Source of All That Is. This is the level of the cosmic energy of Thought/Form that arises out of creative nurturing. The ultimate in ascended mastery is when you know what is going to happen before you act, because you are functioning where thought begins.

"God and Goddess energy are on the same level because Wisdom is needed to balance Understanding, and Understanding is needed to balance Wisdom. You cannot manifest without the creative foundation of being. Being cannot be expressed without the action of manifestation."

Alcyone pauses and I take a deep breath. It's a lot to take in all at once. "Remember, Ignomatius, you came in this way and have mastered each level already. Ascendance is the remembering of your mastery and your spirit. However, today is not your day to ascend. Look up one more time and tell me what you see."

My eyes travel up the trunk. It amazes me that I can see the symbols so easily, they are so high among the branches. My eyes move past the pyramid to the triangle and equal armed cross. Beyond them, a straight line appears in the trunk in a blindingly bright light. I close my eyes but the straight line has been burned into my retina and I see it still.

Alcyone's voice seems to speak from that light as she goes on to explain the next level. "The straight line is Essential spirit: the first division out of Chaos is Intent. This is the creative aspect of All That Is. It is Source or Pure Energy. You see it as light."

She pauses, and even though I do not have my eyes open, I see a circle appear above the straight line. Alcyone seems to know and continues.

"The circle represents All That Is or Chaos. All That Is is just simply that. It is called Chaos because this is the level where pure potential exists, where all the power lies. Liken it to a department store where you can get anything you want, from your morning meal to enlightenment. However, you cannot use it the way it is because it is pure potential. All That Is needs boundaries in order for you to act. It is only with intent that anything happens."

Alcyone goes quiet once more, but it is the silence that contains all the mysteries of the world. I open my eyes to look at her and she has moved into the circle of her sisters. The light that radiates from each sister would feed a human heart hungry for love for a lifetime and beyond. The light pulses around the circle, both within and without. The Pleiades have set their intent. It is time to return to the Light that they are.

Maia turns to Zeus. "Would you give us a step up, my friend?"

Zeus comes to the base of the Tree and kneels with one leg forming the first step up. Maia turns to Poseidon and Prometheus. "Would you ground Ignomatius, so that our friend's soul does not follow us? It is not yet time for Ignomatius to ascend."

Prometheus and Poseidon come to stand beside me. I am feeling a little smothered as I am surrounded by two massive energies, but I stay focused on the Sisters. All is in place for their ascension.

The world around us quiets, almost as if we have stepped out of time and space. For the first time I understand the power of silence. Silence lives all around us, filling up the spaces that no one sees or hears. We rarely stop to listen for it, yet silence is the container for our existence. I watch as the Sisters gather the silence to them. Their silence holds the power of creation, the highest of feminine energy.

Maia looks toward me and bows her head slightly as our final goodbye. She steps forward and places one foot on Zeus's knee. She reaches out and gently touches Zeus's face. Her touch calls forth Zeus's artist soul. His energy for this transition will not be that of the lightening god that all know him to be, but rather, that of the gentle lover and artist.

Maia hesitates before she completes the first step of the journey and turns toward me again. "Enjoy the sunrise for me, Ignomatius. For even as I journey to rejoin my star self, I will hold the glory of sunrise in my soul and know the gift of light as the renewal of each day." Maia turns and steps up and a trail of light flashes through the Tree of Life.

Sterope steps up next. She pays no attention to Zeus as she places her foot upon his knee: he was but a side note to her sojourn here. Instead, she spreads her arms wide and looks to the heavens as if in prayer. "May my journey here leave a trail for all those who are lost and feel abandoned to find their way home." Sterope vanishes into a trail of light after Maia.

Merope steps up next. She places her foot heavily upon Zeus's knee. He winces but does not have the grace to look her in the eye. She speaks to him and her voice holds the thinnest veil of threat. "Zeus, in the future there will be what are called anger management classes. Perhaps you should consider taking one or two since I am sure your karma will keep you bound here for a very long time." Her energy changes completely as a small flower erupts from the earth at her feet, a tribute from Gaia for all her work. She plucks it gently and holds it to her heart and disappears into the trail of light.

Celaeno steps up next and casually places her foot on Zeus's knee. She turns toward me and shifts her form from wolf to vampire to dragon and then back to her human form. "Remember, Ignomatius, there are many intelligent creatures in all forms upon your planet. Do not be blinded by your human hubris. Reach out to them, and they will reach out to you." With a wink at me, she steps into the light.

Taygeta comes forth to take her place at the foot of the Tree of Life. "Remember to call on me when you need me, Ignomatius." With that quick goodbye, she melts into the light. Her trail up the Tree of Life becomes the equation of oneness that holds the universe in formation, a final gift that mathematicians and philosophers will search to discover for lifetimes to come.

Alcyone can barely hold her human form to place her foot on Zeus's knee: stars trail each movement she makes. She looks toward Poseidon, whose energy responds to her as a lover's kiss. It contains an ocean of lovers' goodbyes and regrets for potential loss and joy of union. "I thank you, Ignomatius, for sharing a moment with me as I reflected on my human frailty as a mother. That which I am was expressed in many forms upon the earth. 'Mother' is one that I will leave for another manifestation to master." The Tree of Life practically sings as her passage touches all levels of being on its way home.

Only Electra remains. Zeus pales as she approaches. She starts to raise her right hand and Zeus pales even more. Electra smiles and places her hand upon her heart. She closes her hand around the gift of her heart and turns toward me. As she opens her hand, she gently blows the gift my way. Heart to heart. "Ignomatius, you traveled with me on paths of light and darkness, a trusted companion when all around me looked upon me with disbelief at my audacity. I would gift you with that audacity, but it might get you into more trouble than good. So instead, I gift you and those you serve with the hope of Light returning." As she steps past Zeus into the light, I see a weight lifted from his shoulders.

Again, there was a moment of silence. Gone! They are gone into the light. I press forward to follow the journey that is not mine to take. Poseidon and Prometheus hold me fast.

***

Apollo and Artemis are staring at the waves. Apollo turns to Artemis, "You have waited too long. Even my eye cannot distinguish Orion's head from the waves."

Artemis gives him a withering look. Men have died at the look but Apollo is more resilient. She lifts her bow and arrow and aims as if the shot is only a few yards away. "Goodbye, my friend. May we hunt in the heavens together." She lets the arrow fly and it travels straight to Orion's heart.

***

As we stand in silence at the base of the Tree of Life, Orion bursts from the grove and runs toward Zeus. He leaps off of Zeus's knee into the trail of light left by the Sisters and disappears up into the heavens. I can hear his voice saying, "I never lose my prey."

Apollo appears and he gives Zeus a hearty pat on the back. Then he helps Zeus up from his kneeling position. Being the anchor for the departure of the Seven Sisters has taken a toll on his energy. I watch as the gods congregate around Zeus and know that my time here is done. Zeus turns an eye to me as I fade away. He would smite me if he had a chance. Hopefully, our paths will not cross again.

***

I wake up with the sound of trees moving in the wind outside my window. They say that when a great soul passes, an immense wind blows in tribute. I hear the howling wind and mourn the loss of the Sisters. I will miss them. I get up and look out the window to the night sky and find the familiar constellation, the Pleiades. I stand in silence and mourn, full of wonder and gratitude. I am grateful for having been privileged to witness their passage. The wind howls and my soul weeps.

***

I am sitting with The Hooded One. I have dreaded this moment for days. I am sure she will say our work is done and she, too, will step into the light that is her home. Her question, when it comes, catches me off guard.

"Did you find your God?"

What?

"Did you find your God, Ignomatius?"

I ponder her words as she waits patiently for my answer. I have met gods and goddesses and creatures from legends in my travels. Did I find God? I look to my heart and it is full, where once it was empty. I look at my life and I have meaning and purpose. I look to The Hooded One and see a guide who has filled my life with spiritual richness beyond my wildest imagination. God is not a single entity to be found. The fabric of the universe is made of what we call God and Goddess. We contain that fabric within us, as does all that surrounds us. Yes, I have found God.

"Good, then we can move to other journeys."

You mean there will be more?

"Oh yes, Ignomatius. You and I have lots of journeys to take together, never fear. A good companion and a good cup of tea make the journey worthwhile."

We laugh together over our cup of tea. My heart is overflowing.

Epilogue

The Weaver sits still for a moment, contemplating her weave. The bright passage of the Seven Sisters into the light pulses throughout the strands. Orion's knot moves into a lighter place where the tangles will not affect the Earth plane. Zeus's node was still entangled from his karmic choices. She reaches toward it and then hesitates. Let Zeus work out some of the knots that bound him to form.

She watches the pulsing light of the Sisters again and then reaches ever so gently toward one line of light. She pulls it to her out of the weave.

Electra pops out of the light to stand before her. She looks around and sees The Weaver and realizes where she was. She immediately goes to her knees and bows before The Weaver. It crosses her mind that this might be her final unweaving. None were called before The Weaver in her memory. Yet, she is at peace. Her work will stand for itself.

The Weaver reads her heart like an open book. "You may rise, Electra. It is not time for your final unweaving. However, since you stand in a place of crossroads at the moment, you may choose a totally different path."

Electra rises, but the deference to The Weaver does not leave her posture. "How may I serve?" is her only question.

The Weaver smiles. "Your work with the time lines has impressed me. I will take you on as an apprentice. What do you say to that?"

As the Pleiades settled into the stars in the sky, one winked out, hidden from view.

The End

Appendix

For those who are interested in the various versions of the Pleiades legend, I have included some information from my research.

Directory

Section: A Alycone

Atsma, Aaron J. "Pleiades." *Theoi Project*. 2000-
2017, http://www.theoi.com/Nymphe/NympheAlkyone.html
Accessed (August 14, 2017)

LKYONE (or Alcyone) was a Pleiad star-nymph of Mount
Kithairon (Cithaeron) in Boiotia (central Greece) loved by the
god Poseidon. Her name was interpreted to mean either
"strong-helper" from *alkê + oneô* (*oninêmi*) or "kingfisher"
from*alkyôn*. Bird references can also be found in the name
Peleiades "doves," and Merope the "bee-eater bird" *merops*.

PARENTS
[1.1] ATLAS (Hesiod Astronomy Frag 1, Pausanias 2.31.8)
[1.2] ATLAS & PLEIONE (Apollodorus 3.110, Hyginus Fabulae
192, Hyginus Astronomica 2.21, Ovid Fasti 4.169 & 5.79)
OFFSPRING
[1.1] HYRIEUS, LYKOS, AITHOUSA
(by Poseidon) (Apollodorus 3.110)
[1.2] HYPERES, ANTHAS (by Poseidon) (Pausanias 2.30.8 &
9.22.5)
[1.3] HYRIEUS, EPHOKEUS (by Poseidon) (Hyginus Fabulae
157)

ALCY'ONE or HALCY'ONE (Alkuonê), A Pleiad, a daughter of
Atlas and Pleione, by whom Poseidon begot Aethusa,
Hyrieus and Hyperenor. (Apollod. iii. 10. § 1; Hygin. *Praef.
Fab.* p. 11, ed. Staveren; Ov. *Heroid.*xix. 133.) To these
children Pausanias (ii. 30. § 7) adds two others, Hyperes and
Anthas.

Source: Dictionary of Greek and Roman Biography and
Mythology. This work is in the public domain.

Section B: Celaeno

Atsma, Aaron J. "Pleiades." *Theoi Project*. 2000-2017, http://www.theoi.com/Nymphe/NympheKelaino.html Accessed (August 14, 2017)

KELAINO (or Celaeno) was a Pleiad star-nymph of the island of Euboia or Mount Kithairon (Cithaeron) in Boiotia loved by the god Poseidon. She was probably identified with the nymph Klonie.

PARENTS
[1.1] ATLAS (Hesiod Astronomy Frag 1)
[1.2] ATLAS & PLEIONE (Apollodorus 3.110, Hyginus Fabulae 192, Hyginus Astronomica 2.21, Ovid Fasti 4.169 & 5.79)

Wikipedia contributors. "Lycus (mythology)." *Wikipedia, The Free Encyclopedia*. Wikipedia, The Free Encyclopedia, 14 Jul. 2017. Web. Accessed (August 14, 2017)

OFFSPRING
Lycus, son of Prometheus and Celaeno, brother of Chimaerus. The brothers are said to have had tombs in the Troad; they are otherwise unknown.[5]

Section C: Electra

Atsma, Aaron J. "Pleiades." *Theoi Project*. 2000-2017, http://www.theoi.com/Nymphe/NympheElektra2.html Accessed (August 14, 2017)

ELECTRA (Êlektra), i. e. the bright or brilliant one. A daughter of Atlas and Pleione, was one of the seven Pleiades, and became by Zeus the mother of Jasion and Dardanus. (Apollod. iii. 10. § 1, 12. §§ 1, 3.) According to a tradition preserved in Servius (*ad Aen.* i. 32, ii. 325, iii. 104, vii. 207) she was the wife of the Italian king Corythus, by whom she had a son Jasion; whereas by Zeus she was the mother of Dardanus. (Comp. Serv. *ad Aen.* i. 384, iii. 167; Tzetz. *ad Lycoph.* 29.) Diodorus (v. 48) calls Harmonia her daughter by Zeus. She is connected also with the legend about the Palladium. When Electra, it is said, had come as a suppliant to the Palladium, which Athena had established, Zeus or Athena herself threw it into the territory of Ilium, because it had been sullied by the hands of a woman who was no longer a pure maiden, and king Ilus then built a temple to Zeus. (Apollod. iii. 12. § 3.) According to others it was Electra herself that brought the Palladium to Ilium, and gave it to her son Dardanus. (Schol. *ad Eurip. Phoen.* 1136.) When she saw the city of her son perishing in flames, she tore out her hair for grief and was thus placed among the stars as a comet. (Serv. *ad Aen.* x. 272.) According to others, Electra and her six sisters were placed among the stars as the seven Pleiades, and lost their brilliancy on seeing the destruction of Ilium. (Serv. *ad Virg. Georg.* i. 138; Eustath. *ad Hom.* p. 1155.) The fabulous island of Electris was believed to have received its name from her. (Apollon. Rhod. i. 916.)

Section D: Kartikeya

"Karttikeya." *Encyclopedia Mythica* from Encyclopedia Mythica Online.
<http://www.pantheon.org/articles/k/karttikeya.html>
[Accessed August 14, 2017].

Once an asura (demon) named Taraka performed a great number of austerities for a great number of years and thereby attracted the attention of Brahma. When Brahma asked him what he wanted as reward for his exceptional piety the asura asked for the boon of absolute invulnerability. At this request Brahma was dismayed because Taraka was an asura and not to be trusted with such tremendous power. So the wily god tricked Taraka into accepting a modified boon whereby the asura got absolute invulnerability from every creation in the universe except a son of Shiva. Thus, as a result, nothing and no-one could kill Taraka or overcome him in battle except a son of Shiva. Taraka was overjoyed at even this modified boon as Shiva had no sons and had just lost his wife Sati who had jumped into her father Daksha's funeral fire and been immolated. Shiva was mad with grief and had taken refuge in the forests intent on leading a life of absolute austerity. Taraka thought he had nothing to fear and began what he had initially set out to do, hold absolute sway over all creations in the universe.

So, protected by Brahma's boon, Taraka started extending his domains and not only conquered all creatures on earth but also started making inroads into heaven. He defeated the gods one by one and forced them to pay him tribute. Indra was forced to part with his wonderful white horse, Uchchaisravas, which was one of the fourteen precious things that had turned up at the Churning of the Ocean at the beginning of creation. Jamadagni, the great sage, had to give up his celestial cow Kamdhenu, a creature which could fulfill all desires. Kubera, the god of wealth, had to pay tribute to Taraka in the form of a thousand precious sea-horses and <u>Vayu</u> had to obey all of the wicked asura's commands. Even the sun and the moon were in terror of Taraka and while the sun could not give out any heat the moon was forced to shine all the time. The gods were forced out of their respective heavens and wander about in forests.

One day, in the forests, all the gods gathered in a clearing to discuss how they could overcome Taraka but no way could be found till one of the gods fortunately remembered the lacuna in Brahma's boon to the asura. Taraka was invincible against all except a son of Shiva's. This gave the gods some hope but Shiva was still mourning Sati and living a life of complete celibacy in a forest by Mount Kailash, his usual abode. So the gods began to hatch a plan to persuade Shiva to marry and beget a son. They decided that Sati would be reborn as <u>Parvati</u>, daughter of Himalaya, the mountain. Then they would somehow contrive to marry her off to the still grief-stricken god. So Parvati was born, exceedingly beautiful and worthy of a potent god like Shiva. When she came of age she was made to understand her mission in life and she herself began to perform many austerities in the hope of attracting Shiva's attention but that god was still in grief and impervious to all her best efforts. After the passage of many years without any result Indra began to despair of Parvati's success without some assistance.

So he appointed <u>Kama</u>, the god of love and desire, to go to Mount Kailash and somehow make Shiva break his self-imposed celibacy. That flighty god fearfully went to Kailash and found Shiva deep in meditation, impervious to all around him. Even the birds and animals in that holy place made no noise. Even the leaves on the trees stayed still and made no sound. Kama dared not proceed with what he had been sent to do and hung about the place wondering what he could do.

So Kama dithered about the place quite uncertain as to how to rouse Shiva's desire to wed with Parvati. This uncertain situation went on for many days till, one day, suddenly, Kama saw Parvati approach gently and quietly and start picking flowers to offer to her desired lord, Shiva. Kama immediately saw his opportunity and, setting aside his fear of the hot-tempered god, fitted an arrow to his famed bow and aimed at Shiva and let fly. The arrow flew true to its mark, Shiva's breast. Shiva was rudely shaken out of his meditative trance and his eyes flew open. The first person he saw was the lovely Parvati charmingly picking the colorful flowers. He immediately felt a warm surge of desire for her course through his body. Then he saw Kama and he instantly understood the reason for his unforeseen desire. He flew into a rage at what he thought of as Kama's imprudence and, turning his terrible third eye on that hapless god, reduced him to ashes.

Though now under the influence of physical need for a woman, Shiva was still determined to stick to his life of absolute asceticism. He receded farther into the forests and, ignoring his physical urges, continued with his meditations. Perceiving this, Parvati began anew her austerities in the hope of moving Shiva into noticing her. So this went on for several more years. The gods, exiled to the wildernesses by Taraka's tyranny, yearned for their comfortable heavens but could do nothing in the face of Shiva's obstinacy. At last though, since the potency of one of Kama's arrows never diminishes, Shiva was forced to acknowledge his physical needs and consented to marry Parvati.

The gods were overjoyed at this new development and envisaged that they would soon be able to go back to their old, sybaritic life-styles. Shiva and Parvati wedded amid great pomp and glory and a sumptuous feast to which everyone who was someone was invited was organized to commemorate the auspicious occasion. Yet things were not as they should have been. Many years passed and yet Shiva and Parvati had no issue. The gods fell into consultation again and this time it was decided that Agni, the god of fire, should go to Kailash and find out what was wrong. When Agni reached there, it is fortunate that he perceived Shiva just leaving his wife Parvati. Agni transformed himself into a dove and flew around the place where the two had just been together, he was lucky in finding a seed of Shiva's. He picked this up and made for the place where the other gods waited patiently for his return.

But Agni is a lesser god and he was unable to carry Shiva's seed for long. Soon he grew tired and dropped the seed. It fell on a bank of the river Ganges. There, upon the bank of the great river, arose a child who was beautiful as the moon and brilliant as the sun. As he lay there crying on the bank the six Pleiades, being the daughters of six powerful kings in Hindu myth, came to that very banks to bathe. Seeing the pretty baby lying there without anyone in attendance they were all overcome with motherly love and each offered him her breast. Thus Karttikeya, who was this beautiful child, was suckled simultaneously by six surrogate mothers without much difficulty as, being the son of a god and a god himself, he had six heads and could suckle six breasts all at once.

So Karttikeya grew up in the care of the loving Pleiades and later fulfilled his mission in life, that of killing the tyrannous asura Taraka. Thus the universe was again brought back to the control of the gods who could go back to their heavens and pursue their usual lives of complete leisurely pleasure.

Section E: Maia

Atsma, Aaron J. "Pleiades." *Theoi Project*. 2000-2017, http://www.theoi.com/Nymphe/NympheMaia.html Accessed (August 14, 2017)

MAIA (Maia or Maias), a daughter of Atlas and Pleione (whence she is called Atlantis and Pleias), was the eldest of the Pleiades, and in a grotto of mount Cyllene in Arcadia she became by Zeus the mother of Hermes. Arcas, the son of Zeus by Callisto, was given to her to be reared. (Hom. *Od.* xiv. 435, *Hymn. in Merc.* 3; Hes. *Theog.* 938; Apollod. iii. 10. § 2, 8. § 2; Tzetz. *ad Lycoph.* 219; Horat. *Carm.* i. 10. 1, 2. 42, &c.)

MAIA was the eldest of the Pleiades, the seven nymphs of the constellation Pleiades. She was a shy goddess who dwelt alone in a cave near the peaks of Mount Kyllene (Cyllene0 in Arkadia where she secretly gave birth to a son by Zeus, the god Hermes. She also raised the boy Arkas in her cave, whose mother Kallisto had been transformed into a bear.

Aiskhylos apparently identifies Maia "the nursing mother" with Gaia "the Earth." On several occasions he calls the earth-goddess Gaia Maia (Mother Earth) and pairs her with Hermes Khthonios ("of the Earth").

PARENTS

[1.1] ATLAS (Hesiod Theogony 938, Hesiod Astronomy Frag 1, Homeric Hymn 17.3, Simonides Frag 555, Virgil Aeneid 8.134)

[1.2] ATLAS & PLEIONE (Apollodorus 3.110, Hyginus Fabulae 192, Hyginus Astronomica 2.21, Ovid Fasti 4.169 & 5.79)

OFFSPRING

[1.1] HERMES (by Zeus) (Hesiod Theogony 938, Hesiod Astronomy Frag 1, Homeric Hymns 4& 17, Alcaeus Frag 308, Simonides Frag 555, Aeschylus Libation Bearers 683 & Frag 212, Apollodorus 3.112, Philostratus Elder 1.26, Ovid Fasti 5.79)

Section F: Merope

Atsma, Aaron J. "Pleiades." *Theoi Project*. 2000-2017, http://www.theoi.com/Nymphe/NympheMerope.html Accessed (August 14, 2017)

MEROPE was one of the seven Pleiades, star-nymph daughters of the Titan Atlas. She married the impious king Sisyphos (Sisyphus) and was ancestress of the Korinthian (Corinthian) and Lykian (Lycian) royal families. Merope was said to have been so ashamed of her husband's crimes that she hid her face amongst the stars of heaven, and so the seventh star of the Pleiades faded away from human sight.

Her name is variously interpreted to mean "with face turned" from *meros + ops*, "with sparkling face" (*mar*)*mairô + ops*, and "bee-eater bird" *merops*. The first etymology was derived from the fading of the star, the second is a typically starry name--cf. Maira, the dog-star--, while the third reflects the connection of the Pleiades--who were also known as Peleiades or "doves"--with birds.

PARENTS

[1.1] ATLAS (Hesiod Astronomy Frag 1)

[1.2] ATLAS & PLEIONE (Apollodorus 3.110, Hyginus Fabulae 192, Hyginus Astronoicay 2.21, Ovid Fasti 4.169 & 5.79)

OFFSPRING

[1.1] GLAUKOS (by Sisyphos) (Apollodorus 1.85, Hyginus Astronomica 2.21)

ME'ROPE (Meropê). A daughter of Atlas, one of the Pleiades, and the wife of Sisyphus of Corinth, by whom she became the mother of Glaucus. In the constellation of the Pleiades she is the seventh and the least visible star, because she is ashamed of having had intercourse with a mortal man. (Apollod. i. 9. § 3, iii. 10. 1; Ov. *Fast.* iv. 175; Eustath. *ad Hom.* p. 1155; Serv. *ad Virg. Geory.* i. 138; comp. Hom. *Il.* vi. 154; Schol.*ad Pind. Nem.* ii. 16.)

Source: Dictionary of Greek and Roman Biography and Mythology.

Aeschylus, Sisyphus the Runaway (lost play) (Greek tragedy C5th B.C.)
Weir Smyth (L.C.L.) quotes Pherecydes, a C5th B.C. mythographer, in his discussion of the plot of this lost play: "*Sisyphos drapetês* (the Runaway) was satyric; its theme, the escape from Haides of the crafty Korinthian king. According to the fabulous story told by Pherekydes (Frag. 78 in Müller, *Fragmenta Historicum Graecorum*) . . . Before he died Sisyphos directed his wife Merope to omit his funeral rites, so that Haides, being deprived of his customary offerings, was persuaded by the cunning trickster to let him go back to life in order to complain of his wife's neglect. But, once in the upper world, he refused to return, and had to be fetched back by Hermes.'"

Source: Dictionary of Greek and Roman Biography and Mythology.

Section G: Orion

Atsma, Aaron J. "Pleiades." *Theoi Project*. 2000-2017, http://www.theoi.com/Gigante/GiganteOrion.html Accessed (August 14, 2017)

ORION was a handsome giant gifted with the ability to walk on water by his father Poseidon. He served King Oinopion of Khios (Chios) as huntsman for a time, but was blinded and exiled from the island after raping the king's daughter Merope. Orion then travelled across the sea to Lemnos and petitioned the god Hephaistos for help in recovering his sight. Lending him his assistant Kedalion, the god directed the giant travel to the rising place of the sun, where the sun-god would restore his vision. Upon returning to Greece, Orion sought out Oinopion, but the king hid himself in an underground bronze chamber to avoid retribution.

After this the giant retired to the island of Delos or Krete and became a hunting companion of the goddess Artemis. He died while in her service and was placed amongst the stars as the constellation Orion. The circumstances of his death are variously related. In one version he desired to marry the goddess but her brother Apollo tricked Artemis into shooting him with an arrow as he was swimming far out at sea. In another version, Artemis killed him deliberately after he raped her attendant Oupis. However the most common story was that Orion bragged he would hunt down all the beasts of the earth, and so Mother Earth sent up a giant scorpion to destroy him. Both the giant and scorpion were placed amongst the stars, one rising as the other set.

Finally the Boiotians had their own set of myths associated with the hunter of the constellation. According to their version Orion was born when the three gods; Zeus, Poseidon and Hermes urinated on a bull-hide and buried it in the earth to provide King Hyrieus with a son. The boy was named Orion after the urine, but was also known by the name of Kandaon. His son and daughters were heroes who died for the town of Thebes.

PARENTS

[1.1] POSEIDON & EURYALE (Hesiod Astronomy Frag 4, Pherecydes Frag, Apollodorus 1.25, Hyginus Astronomica 2.34)

[1.2] POSEIDON (Valerius Flaccus 4.104)

[2.1] GAIA (Apollodorus 1.25)

[2.2] HYRIEOS (Parthenius 20, Antoninus Liberalis 25)

[2.3] Born of GAIA & an oxhide soaked with the urine of ZEUS, POSEIDON, & HERMES (Hyginus Fabulae 195 & Astr 2.34, Ovid Fasti 5.493, Servius ad Aeneid 10.763, Nonnus Dionysiaca 13.96)

[3.1] OINOPION (Servius on Virgil's Aeneid 10.763)

OFFSPRING

[1.1] 50 x sons (by the Kephisides) (Corinna Frag 655)

[2.1] THE KORONIDES (Antoninus Liberalis 25, Ovid Metamorphoses 13.685)

[3.1] DRYAS (Statius Thebaid 7.255)

ORI'ON (Oriôn), a son of Hyrieus, of Hyria, in Boeotia, a very handsome giant and hunter, and said to have been called by the Boeotians Candaon. (Hom. *Od.* xi. 309; Strab. ix. p. 404; Tzetz. *ad Lyc.* 328.) Once he came to Chios (Ophiusa), and fell in love with Aero, or Merope, the daughter of Oenopion, by the nymph Helice. He cleared the island from wild beasts, and brought the spoils of the chase as presents to his beloved; but as Oenopion constantly deferred the marriage, Orion one day being intoxicated forced his way into the chamber of the maiden. Oenopion now implored the assistance of Dionysus, who caused Orion to be thrown into a deep sleep by satyrs, in which Oenopion blinded him. Being informed by an oracle that he should recover his sight, if he would go towards the east and expose his eye-balls to the rays of the rising sun, Orion following the sound of a Cyclops' hammer, went to Lemnos, where Hephaestus gave to him Cedalion as his guide. When afterwards he had recovered his sight, Orion returned to Chios to take vengeance, but as

Oenopion had been concealed by his friends, Orion was unable to find him, and then proceeded to Crete, where he lived as a hunter with Artemis. (Apollod. i. 4. § 3; Parthen. *Erot.* 20; Theon, *ad Arat.* 638 ; Hygin. *Poet. Astr.* ii. 34.) The cause of his death, which took place either in Crete or Chios, is differently stated. According to some Eos, who loved Orion for his beauty, carried him off, but as the gods were angry at this, Artemis killed him with an arrow in Ortygia (Hom. *Od.* v. 121); according to others he was beloved by Artemis, and Apollo, indignant at his sister's affection for him, asserted that she was unable to hit with her bow a distant point which he showed to her in the sea. She thereupon took aim, and hit it, but the point was the head of Orion, who had been swimming in the sea. (Hygin. l. c.; Ov. *Fast.* v. 537.) A third account states that he harboured an improper love for Artemis, that he challenged her to a game of discus, or that he violated Upis, on which account Artemis shot him, or sent a monstrous scorpion which killed him. (Serv. *ad Aen.* i. 539 ; Horat. *Carm.* ii. 4. 72; Apollod. i. 4.§ 5.) A fourth account, lastly, states that he boasted he would conquer every animal, and would clear the earth from all wild beasts; but the earth sent forth a scorpion by which he was killed. (Ov. *Fast.* v. 539, &c.) Asclepius wanted to recall him to life, but was slain by Zeus with a flash of lighting. The accounts of his parentage and birth-place are varying in the different writers, for some call him a son of Poseidon and Euryale (Apollod, i. 4. § 3), and others say that he was born of the earth, or a son of Oenopion. (Serv. *ad Aen.* i. 539, x. 763.) He is further called a Theban, or Tanagraean, but probably because Hyria, his native place, sometimes belonged to Tanagra, and sometimes to Thebes. (Hygin. *Poet. Astr.* ii. 34; Paus. ix. 20 § 3; Strab. ix. p. 404.) After his death, Orion was placed among the stars (Hom. *Il.* xviii. 486, &c., xxii. 29, *Od.* v. 274), where he appears as a giant with a girdle, sword, a lion's skin and a club. As the rising and setting of the constellation of Orion was believed to be accompanied by storms and rain, he is often called *imbrifer, nimbosus,* or *aquosus.* His tomb was shown at Tanagra. (Paus. ix. 20.& 3.)

Source: Dictionary of Greek and Roman Biography and Mythology.

Section H: Pleiades

Atsma, Aaron J. "Pleiades." *Theoi Project*. 2000-2017, www.theoi.com/Nymphe/NymphaiPleiades.html. Accessed (August 14, 2017)

PLEIADES (Pleiades or Peleiades), the Pleiads, are called daughters of Atlas by Pleione (or by the Oceanid Aethra, Eustath. *ad Hom.* p. 1155), or Erechtheus (Serv. *ad Aen.* i. 744), of Cadmus (Theon, *ad. Arat.* p. 22), or of the queen of the Amazons. (Schol. *ad Theocrit.* xiii. 25.) They were the sisters of the Hyades, and seven in number, six of whom are described as visible, and the seventh as invisible. Some call the seventh Sterope, and relate that she became invisible from shame, because she alone among her sisters had had intercourse with a mortal man ; others call her Electra, and make her disappear from the choir of her sisters on account of her grief at the destruction of the house of Dardanus (Hygin. *Fab. 192, Poet. Astr.* ii. 21). The Pleiades are said to have made away with themselves from grief at the death of their sisters, the Hyades, or at the fate of their father, Atlas, and were afterwards placed as stars at the back of Taurus, where they form a cluster resembling a bunch of grapes, whence they were sometimes called botrus (Eustath. *ad Hom.* p. 1155). According to another story, the Pleiades were virgin companions of Artemis, and, together with their mother Pleione, were pursued by the hunter Orion in Boeotia; their prayer to be rescued from him was heard by the gods, and they were metamorphosed into doves (peleiades), and placed among the stars (Hygin.*Poet. Astr.* ii. 21; Schol. *ad Apollon. Rhod.* iii. 226; Pind. *Nem.* ii. 17). The rising of the Pleiades in Italy was about the beginning of May, and their setting about the beginning of November. Their names are Electra, Maia, Taygete, Alcyone, Celaeno, Sterope, and Merope (Tzetz. *ad Lyc.* 219, comp. 149; Apollod. iii. 10. § 1). The scholiast of Theocritus (xiii. 25) gives the following different set of names : Coccymo, Plaucia,

Protis, Parthemia, Maia, Stonychia, Lampatho. (Comp.
Hom. *Il.* xviii. 486, *Od.* v. 272; Ov. *Fast.* iv. 169, &c.; Hyades;
and Ideler, *Untersuch. über die Sternennamen,* p. 144.

175

Section I: Sterope

Atsma, Aaron J. "Pleiades." *Theoi Project*. 2000-
2017, http://www.theoi.com/Nymphe/NympheSterope.html
Accessed (August 14, 2017)

STEROPE (or Asterope) was a Pleiad star-nymph of Pisa in Elis (southern Greece). She was loved STE'ROPE (Steropê). A Pleiad, the wife of Oenomaus (Apollod. iii. 10. § 1), and according to Pausanias (v. 10. § 5), a daughter of Atlas. by the god Ares and bore him Oinomaos.

Sterope was probably identified with the Naiad Harpina who is otherwise named as the mother of Oinomaos by Ares.

PARENTS[1.1] ATLAS (Hesiod Astronomy Frag 1)

[1.2] ATLAS & PLEIONE (Apollodorus 3.110, Hyginus Fabulae 192, Hyginus Astronomica 2.21, Ovid Fasti 4.169 & 5.79)

OFFSPRING

[1.1] OINOMAOS (by Ares) (Hyginus Fabulae 84, Hyginus Astronomica 2.21)

[1.2] OINOMAOS, EUENOS (by Ares) (Plutarch Greek & Roman Parallel Stories 38)

Source: Dictionary of Greek and Roman Biography and Mythology.

Section J: Taygeta

Atsma, Aaron J. "Pleiades." *Theoi Project*. 2000-2017, http://www.theoi.com/Nymphe/NympheTaygete.html Accessed (August 14, 2017)

TAYGETE was the Pleiad star and mountain nymph of the Taygetos Mountains in Lakedaimonia (Laconia), southern Greece. She was loved by Zeus. Their son Lakedaimon (Lacedaemon) was the ancestor of the kings of Sparta.

PARENTS
[1.1] ATLAS (Hesiod Astronomy Frag 1)
[1.2] ATLAS & PLEIONE (Apollodorus 3.110, Hyginus Fabulae 192, Hyginus Astronomica 2.21, Ovid Fasti 4.169 & 5.79)
OFFSPRING
[1.1] LAKEDAIMON (by Zeus) (Apollodorus 3.116, Pausanias 3.12, Hyginus Fabulae 155 & Astronomica 2.21, Nonnus Dionysiaca 32.65)

TAY'GETE (Taügetê), a daughter of Atlas and Pleione, one of the Pleiades. (Apollod. iii. 10. § 1.) By Zeus she became the mother of Lacedaemon (Apollod. iii. 10. § 3; Paus. iii. 1. § 2, 18. § 7, 20. § 2) and of Eurotas. (Steph. Byz. *s. v.* Taygeton.) Mount Taygetus, in Laconia, derived its name from her. (Schol. *ad Eurip. Or. 615.*) According to some traditions, Taygete refused to yield to the embraces of Zeus, and in order to secure her against him, Artemis metamorphosed her into a cow. Taygete showed her gratitude towards Artemis by dedicating to her the Cerynitian hind with golden antlers. (Schol. *ad Pind. Ol.* iii. 53.) Some traditions, moreover, state that by Tantalus she became the mother of Pelops. (Hygin. *Fab. 82.*)

Source: Dictionary of Greek and Roman Biography and Mythology.

Section K: Wurrunnah

http://www.sacred-texts.com/aus/mla/mla03.htm Accessed (August 14, 2017)

The Story of the Seven Sisters and the Faithful Lovers

In the dream time, many ages ago, the cluster of stars which we now know as the Pleiades, or the Seven Sisters, were seven beautiful ice maidens. Their parents were a great rugged mountain whose dark head was hidden in the clouds, and an ice-cold stream that flowed from the snow-clad hills. The Seven Sisters wandered across the land, with their long hair flying behind them like storm clouds before the breeze. Their cheeks were flushed with the kiss of the sun, and in their eyes was hidden the soft, grey light of the dawn. So entrancing was their beauty that all men loved them, but the maidens' affections were as cold as the stream which gave them birth, and they never turned aside in their wanderings to gladden the hearts of men.

One day a man named Wurrunnah, by a cunning device, captured two of the maidens, and forced them to live with him, while their five sisters travelled to their home in the sky. When Wurrunnah discovered that the sisters whom he had captured were ice-maidens, whose beautiful tresses were like the icicles that drooped from the trees in winter time, he was disappointed. So he took them to a camp fire, and endeavored to melt the cold crystals from their beautiful limbs. But, as the ice melted, the water quenched the fire, and he succeeded only in dimming their icy brightness.

The two sisters were very lonely and sad in their captivity, and longed for their home in the clear blue sky. When the shadow of night was over the land, they could see their five sisters beckoning to them as they twinkled afar off. One day Wurrunnah told them to gather pine-bark in the forest. After a short journey, they came to a great pine tree, and commenced to strip the bark from it. As they did so, the pine tree (which belonged to the same totem as the maidens) extended itself to the sky. The maidens took advantage of this friendly act, and climbed to the home of their sisters. But they never regained their original brightness, and that is the reason why there are five bright stars and two dim ones in the group of the Pleiades. The Seven Sisters have not forgotten the earth folk. When the snow falls softly they loose their wonderful tresses to the caress of the breeze, to remind us of their journey across our land.

When the Seven Sisters were on earth, of all the men who loved them the Berai Berai, or two brothers, were the most faithful. When they hunted in the forest, or waited in the tall reeds for the wild ducks, they always brought the choicest morsels of the chase as an offering to the Sisters. When the maidens wandered far across the mountains, the Berai Berai followed them, but their love was not favored.

When the maidens set out on their long journey to the sky, the Berai Berai were grieved, and said: "Long have we loved you and followed in your footsteps, O maidens of the dawn, and, when you have left us' we will hunt no more." And they laid aside their weapons and mourned for the maidens until the dark shadow of death fell upon them. When they died, the fairies pitied them, and placed them in the sky, where they could hear the Sisters singing. Thus were they happily rewarded for their constancy. On a starry night, you will see them listening to the song of the Seven Sisters. We call them Orion's Sword and Belt, but it is a happier thought to remember them as the faithful lovers who have listened to the song of the stars from the birth of time.

About the author:

Retta Flagg lives in Virginia Beach with her partner, Crystal Doll, sister, Katie the Golden Doodle, and a reincarnating plant, which we think is a Dieffenbachia. Her spiritual adventures started early in life growing up in Maine where she enjoyed talking to trees and lakes.

She discovered existentialism in college and after surviving her first existential crisis, she converted to goddess worship. She led an ongoing full moon circle for over ten years. The Seth books were the first time she read a world view that explained the nature of reality in a way that made sense to her. Having read several books by a trance channeler, she jumped at the opportunity to see one live and in person when Lea Schultz came to Pittsburgh and channeled a being named Samuel in 1986 https://discoversamuel.com.

Since that time, she has traveled the world with the Samuel group doing high ritual and meditation at sacred places such as Uluru in Australia, Lake Titicaca in Bolivia, temples in Egypt, and the Yangtze River in China. The spiritual teachings and practices in this book come primarily from her studies with Samuel.

You may want to see some of her great travel pictures on her website www.rettaflagg.com.